A Christmas Kiss

AN EASTON FAMILY CHRISTMAS

JEN GEIGLE JOHNSON

Follow Jen

Jen's other published books

The Nobleman's Daughter
Two lovers in disguise

Scarlet
The Pimpernel retold

A Lady's Maid
Can she love again?

His Lady in Hiding
Hiding out at his maid.

Spun of Gold
Rumpelstilskin Retold

Dating the Duke
Time Travel: Regency man in NYC

Charmed by His Lordship
The antics of a fake friendship

Tabitha's Folly
Four over-protective brothers

To read Damen's Secret
The Villain's Romance

Follow her Newsletter

Lords for the Sisters of Sussex Series

The Duke's Second Chance

The Earl's Winning Wager

Her Lady's Whims and Whimsies

Suitors for the Proper Miss

Pining for Lord Lockhart

The Foibles and Follies of Miss Grace

Follow Jen's Newsletter for a free book and to stay up to date on her releases. https://www.subscribepage.com/y8p6z9

Chapter One

Evaline carefully wrapped a black band around her arm. "Remy, could you help me tie it tight enough that it will stay?"

"Certainly, my lady." Her loyal lady's maid cinched it and applied a pin at the back for good measure.

"Excellent. Mother deserves longer than the small three hundred and sixty five days of mourning no matter what Father or Aunt say."

"Yes, my lady." Remy seemed to have sympathy. It was so difficult to tell what went through the woman's mind. But Eva chose to interpret her most uttered three words, "yes, my lady," with whichever emotion Eva desired to hear at the moment, and that is precisely why she and Remy got on so well.

The rest of her clothing flowed around her in anything but mourning colors. Mother forgive her, but she must forge ahead. Her gown of bright canary yellow would glow even in the darker lighting of Almack's. Her hair was tall and wrapped in a turban adorned with a full array of peacock feathers. Her gloves were a bright purple. Her slippers green. She applied rouge, enough that people would know she'd done it, and though she hoped to take further steps outside of acceptable fashion in the future, her current dress seemed garish enough for her first party out of mourning.

She determined never to ever attract another man again, for money or otherwise. If she was ridiculous enough, perhaps they would have no desire to ask father for her hand. And, the other reason shook around uncomfortably inside, the sharp points pokey and injurious. If she was loud enough in her clothing choices, perhaps they wouldn't notice anything else about her either. No matter, she planned to refuse any other offer of marriage regardless of what they noticed.

The soft wood of her floors, the familiar creeks along the hall connecting the family rooms led her to pause in the doorway to her mother's bedchamber. It no longer smelled of her unless she walked among the clothing. But she whispered in to the darkness. "I love you, Mother."

Her aunt waited at the bottom of the stairs and clucked when Eva came into view. She shook her head. "Child." The tone alone could have intimidated a lesser female.

Eva's chin rose higher.

Her father joined Aunt, eyed Eva for a moment and then nodded. And that was all that needed to be said today. Eva swept past her aunt and her disapproving glares, and allowed the servant to drape a shawl across her shoulders. It was exquisite, and gemmed, with a beautiful reflective quality in the fabric. She turned to her father.

"A gift."

She curtseyed. "Thank you."

"You look beautiful."

She dipped her head again, wishing she could believe him, and rested a hand on his forearm. The plush of the carriage seat enveloped her. She ran her gloved hand along the lovely velvet, watching it change color depending on the direction of her movement.

As she expected, no one said much of anything in the carriage. At one point, she braved an oft repeated complaint. "I don't know why we are attending Almack's since we know I will accept no one's hand."

Aunt sniffed. "We must make our appearances. The longer we continue as if all is normal, the more likely they will forget your…em…indiscretion."

Eva didn't respond. The conversation had become tired, overused, almost unheard at this point.

But as they were about to arrive, father placed a hand on her arm. "I am thinking of your mother." The pain in his eyes flickered a moment, and she had to swallow twice before an uncomfortable sharpness eased. "I as well." It was their way, to mention mother now and again. Perhaps they clung to her memory in hopes that no one would let her go. Perhaps it just helped them feel connected. Mother was the one thing that made them a family.

A footman helped her down, and then she and her aunt each took one of her father's arms and they approached Almack's together. Her breathing picked up, the entrance looming ahead of her, people's gazes on her. She couldn't tell if they were curious or wished her ill. And then she remembered her clothing. Of course people were staring. She lifted her chin. She could do this. Let them stare at her clothing. That's why she wore it. Memories of the last time she walked through those doors tried to crowd in, but she pushed them aside. She was a new person now. She reached for her single black band of mourning and allowed her breaths to strengthen her.

They presented their vouchers, and then a footman announced them to the room. "Lord Hollings. Lady Eva, and Mrs. Wickers."

They bowed or curtseyed to the room, all the while Eva commanding her knees to be still. So far she daren't look at a single face. But her father's arm was strong, and she felt stronger. She braved a peak. Women were eyeing her turban. Some touched their own hair.

Eva smiled. Perfect. She walked into the room. Soon they were surrounded. Many women vying for her father's attention surprised her. She stepped away, slightly, but then realized they were equally vying for her own.

"Lady Evaline. You have chosen the absolute perfect feathers." Did the vaguely familiar woman laugh behind her hand when she said it?

"Thank you." Eva looked from face to face. "These are a particular kind of peacock."

Their attention drifted. So, did they not wish to converse? Not really?

The music had started up. Her father asked a particularly young woman to dance and Eva found it difficult to swallow again. This would have been her mother's first set. But her father seemed happy. He smiled and laughed. She could not begrudge him happiness.

The room was full of people. The conversations all blended together, the dresses were white with some splashes of color mixed in. Hers of course was the most bold, the brightest.

A man approached and bowed. "Perhaps you will not remember me?" His chestnut curls were charming, his warm brown eyes comforting. He was tall, broad, thick in his breeches. The man could have been any number of the Corinthians she saw about.

He looked vaguely familiar. She shook her head.

"I am Mr. Oscar Easton. Would you like to dance?" Something about his voice flowed through her like a delicious honey.

Aunt nodded at her as though to demand she dance. The man looked pleasant enough, certainly handsome. She was about to accept him, but her attention was caught by movement. A group of men slightly behind him were watching, speaking behind their hands, perhaps in league with this man. A sharp sense of hurt pounded in her heart. Eva shook her head. "I don't believe I shall." She curtseyed and then moved past him, ignoring her aunt's gasp and whatever she might say to the young man.

She ignored the men who were now undoubtedly laughing and saw only one chair in the corner. If she could just make it there…

But a familiar voice stopped her. "Lady Eva, is that you?"

Eva's shoulder's stiffened. *Miss Penny.* Would that she could avoid this woman altogether. Eva turned. Miss Penny rested her hands at the elbow of a tall Lord. Another stood waiting with a hopeful expression.

"Lady Eva, might I present Lord Stanhope to you?"

"You might."

He bowed. "Would you like to dance?"

At this second request, with more witnesses, Eva had no choice. She nodded, though out of the corner of her eye, saw Mr. Easton who she'd just denied. She, Penny, her partner and Lord Stanhope joined the line, ready to begin a fast paced country dance.

Mr. Easton had also found a partner. She felt a portion of relief at that.

She worked her way through the line and even managed to enjoy herself, but toward the end, the band on her arm started to slip. The room was overly warm. Her turban weighed on her. Now and again a feather fell forward and tickled her face. More than anything, she wished for a moment outside on the cooler verandah.

But no cool moment was in her near future. This particular dance seemed as though it would go on forever. She moved to the center, took Lord Stanhope's hands and with him, shuffled down the middle. Her band slipped further. She wished to push it back up again but it now rested almost at her wrist. They spun in circles and then as she raised an arm high, the band flung off and sailed across the room.

Open mouthed, she watched it head for the lemonade table in one long smooth arch and was intercepted by Mr. Easton, the man to whom she had declined a dance. He and his partner were the last two in line at the moment which placed them close to the lemonade table. With his face full of humor, he nodded once and then pocketed her band.

She almost walked off the floor toward him, but Lord Stanhope stepped forward again and moved to circle around her. Mr. Easton disappeared from view. Certain she looked a sight, with turban beginning to slip, feathers drooping, her hair wet with perspiration, Eva continued the dance until the end, ready to make a bee line for the ladies receiving room and then home.

Her farewell curtsey was as short as allowed. She placed a hand on Lord Stanhope's arm and asked to be led in the direction of the ladies' exit.

"I really enjoyed our dance." His voice murmured to her in a possible attempt at something romantic?

"Yes, thank you." She longed to begin re-wrapping her turban as she made her way across the floor.

"I would like to come calling."

"Certainly." She hardly heard.

"And wonder if I might speak to your father."

She choked. "Wait, you wish to speak with my father?" She stopped walking. Someone nearly ran into her.

Unphased by her surprise, he nodded. "If I could have the honor, yes."

She studied him. "We don't know each other."

"Not yet. I feel a courtship might enable such a thing to occur." He adjusted his sleeves.

His pompous attitude about the whole thing was beginning to needle at her. "And what about me do you find so appealing after a singular dance that you wish to align yourself so closely?" She raised an eyebrow.

He opened his mouth and then closed it. "You are so bold."

She waited.

"I find you…your turban, your dress, ehm, I enjoyed our dance." The man stammered about until he then wisely stopped.

"Speaking with my father won't be necessary." She turned from him. "Thank you for our dance." She continued a much quicker pace to the door. But before she could reach its sanctuary, Miss Penny's voice again stopped her. "Lady Evaline?"

With a groan she turned but then froze on the spot. Miss Penny had another Lord beside her. "Might I have this dance?" He bowed.

Her turban slipped further. In another minute, it would

be down over one eye. Miss Penny eyed it with a sort of crooked enjoyment.

Eva narrowed her eyes.

The music started, and this new Lord was waiting for her response. She opened her mouth, certain she would have to accept, but then Mr. Easton approached. "There you are."

She turned to him and placed a hand on his proffered arm. "Pardon me?"

"We have this next set, but I wondered if you might wish for a moment of cooler air first?" He indicated the verandah.

"Oh, thank you, yes." She turned to the Lord still waiting. "I could reserve you another."

He nodded but she left on Mr. Easton's arm before further arrangements could be made. Unsure how to respond to Mr. Easton, she continued at his side, hoping the turban would halt in its course down her face.

He said nothing until he diverted their course suddenly and moved behind a rather large and bushy plant.

"What are you doing?" Confused, trying not to be alarmed, she raised a hand to her turban to steady it's fall.

"I feel your turban could use some readjusting." He indicated her head.

"Yes, certainly, but perhaps we could continue outside?"

"If we do, then more will see me assist you with such things."

"You know how to help a lady with her turban?" She stepped closer indicating he might try.

"It cannot be too complicated. Now come. Let us adjust this here." He studied her head, unpinning here and there and then tugged out some of the turban before wrapping it snuggly against her head. "There." He placed a few more

8

pins. "You will need to ask for finishing touches from the ladies in the receiving room but at least now it will not fall to the floor in a heap of fabric and feathers."

She studied him, unsure what to say. "Thank you."

"You're welcome."

Now even more guilty of assuming ill of him. "I denied you our dance."

He nodded.

For some reason, it seemed right to confess all. "The others are laughing at me."

He didn't answer for a moment. "I think they are, yes." He cleared his throat. "However, I think you are now in no danger from your turban. Would you care for an escort to the receiving room?"

"Might we take a stroll outside?" She was drawn to him. She somehow suspected that if she were to depart his company, nothing would be as pleasant as she felt right in that moment.

"What if your turban falls? Do you trust my ministrations to that degree?"

"I think I might. Or I care very little." She patted her turban. "I think it will stay."

"Then certainly. Allow me?"

She nodded and took his arm. "I'm astounded at your gentlemanly nature."

"Your astonishment makes me embarrassed for my sex."

"Nevertheless. You have proven a rare and welcome find."

He started to bow his gratitude, but she interrupted. "One I will never marry."

He choked. "Excuse me?"

"I won't marry you."

"Have I proposed and not noticed?" His grin lifted, obviously highly amused.

"Not at all. But I'd like that understood before we begin any semblance of a friendship."

"Ah, and are you considering such an alliance with me?" He dipped his head. "I don't call one a friend, lightly."

"Nor I." She pressed her mouth together. "It is left to be seen, but at least we understand each other in all marriage considerations."

"Most definitely, for I am not looking to get married."

"Singular." She didn't really believe him.

"How so?"

"A man, not looking to get married?" She folded her arms.

"There are a great many just like me, I'm afraid."

"But not a great many who seek me out. Most of those are the marrying kind, *I'm* afraid."

They approached the doors to exit. The cool air refreshed her immediately. She held her arms out. "This is lovely."

"Much better, I agree."

The night air was cool. The moon rose higher in the sky. Now and then a star twinkled, still visible even with candle light closer to her view. The gardens down below looked inviting. But their space on the verandah would have to do.

He stood beside her, a respectable distance. "Tell me, Lady Eva, how you come to be wearing such an immense adornment on your head."

She laughed and then shrugged. "I was attempting to show a bit of height."

"You succeeded." He stood at eye level with the top part of her turban.

"How does it look from your viewpoint?"

"Most excellent, naturally. I appreciate that you do have hair in there. That was comforting."

"Oh? Can you see my hair?"

"Every now and then."

She nodded. "I'm happy to hear that."

"It's a lovely color."

"What is? The Feathers?"

"No, well, yes. The feathers have beautiful colors, but I was talking about your hair."

She paused a moment in their walk and placed a hand at her heart. "Thank you. I don't often hear such things from others."

"How could you not?"

"I don't know how to answer, as I don't know the minds of others, but they seem to find me, less than ideal."

"If that is true, it is a crime."

"Nevertheless…" She wanted to change the subject but didn't know how. As much as she'd love to hear more from him about how others should admire her, she knew it would be a stretch to pull more such thoughts from him. So she stared out at the gardens in silence, contented to feel the cooler air.

"Tell me more of your estate."

"Why? You wish to know if it would suit?" She wanted to bite back the words but she didn't, and now she couldn't take them back. Here, a man was being kind, a man who'd she'd dreadfully insulted, and she had gone and insulted him yet again.

But he just chuckled. "Still determined to believe I'm after your hand?"

"I'm sorry."

"Let's talk of something else then. If not your estate, what interests you?"

"We can talk of my estate. We live near a village, as most estates do, and the children there have a school. I've spent many hours there, with the children. It's fun to teach them things."

"What do you teach them?"

"Reading, their numbers, some of them, more advanced things." She turned to him. "I fill in where the professor needs me."

She found she enjoyed talking to Mr. Easton, more than any other man of her acquaintance, more than the women as well. He had an easy way about him. And even though she knew he might not stay close this season, surely he had other women to woo, she was grateful for this small respite. They talked of lovely things. She learned he loved horses and she shared that she would love to ride. They set up an outing in the park in a few days. For a short moment, Eva forgot that she was uncomfortable or supposed to be avoiding men at all costs. And even if she'd remembered more clearly, now and again, she knew most certainly that Mr. Easton was not looking to get married. And that made him the perfect friend. But as he talked with great animation of his family, four other brothers, and his eyes lit, his mouth curling in a soft smile when he mentioned his sister, Tabitha, she knew she should be afraid indeed if she were to maintain her stance of never another man in her life.

Chapter Two

M r. Oscar Easton left Lady Evaline to herself after a most engaging conversation out on the verandah, one that took the time of two full dances. He'd have to thank her later. He loved a good ball, but this particular ball was becoming more tiresome than others. It seemed that every woman there was seeking for the titled, the wealthy, the famous, and he was none of those. A second son such as he, with nothing to offer but his charm left much to be desired among the typical crowd at Almack's. And yet, he'd attended to appease his father, the man who was no longer with them. Oscar knew he would be happiest if his boys married, were he alive. He would make an effort to settle himself. He must.

His brother approached, looking more self-assured than ever. "That was a good selection."

"Ah, the heir." He lifted a glass of lemonade in his direction. "Good to see you brother."

"Stop with that and listen to me. Lady Evaline, that was a good move."

"What are you talking about?"

"She's worth well over sixty thousand pounds."

Oscar choked. "I wish you hadn't told me that."

"Why ever not?"

"Because I enjoyed her company. I don't want to be looking at her and remember such a vulgar conversation."

"Hm. Well, you know that were he still here, father would be about out of patience with your delay in choosing a wife. A barrister? A military commission? Perhaps the clergy?"

"You tire me. I got this enough from him."

"Fine, consider your options and the far lovelier of all stands right there in this very room."

When Oscar refused to engage in this particular conversation, Edward lifted his hands in the air. "I'll take my attentions to the woman who appreciates them."

"You do just that, thank you."

His brother made his way to the woman he wished to marry. They were all but official, and Oscar was happy for them. Perhaps one day he would be so blessed.

Oscar spent the rest of the time at Almack's vaguely aware of this singular woman. Eva turned most men down. And yet others still sought her out. Her bright yellow gown was the only of its kind in all of the room. She was only passably friendly to most. Her father danced with many. Her aunt hovered about certainly but left her be. He looked forward to their ride so that he might sketch out her character more fully.

When the time came for them to at last be out on horses, he was disappointed that she hurried to stand on the block to help herself up. Perhaps she would require assistance to dismount.

Days past. Their ride came and went, and he understood her no better than he had at the first. Today they were to visit a museum. She had suggested they walk. But when he arrived, the rain came down in sheets. He stood with an umbrella at her doorway.

She exited with her maid and he led them quickly to the equipage.

Once inside he shrugged. "Perhaps we can walk next time?"

"Next time?"

"Certainly. Do you think we will discover all the delights to such a place after one visit?"

"Of course not, but Mr. Easton. If you continue to pay visits as you are, people will consider you besotted or after my dowry." Her eyes narrowed for a moment but then she simply sat still and waited for a response.

"I'm certainly not besotted!" He snorted. And then regretted the moment of hurt that passed across her face. "But you're not either."

"Tis true." She admitted.

"And I'm not after your dowry."

"Why not?" Her confused frown was almost amusing.

"Because I don't think that's a good enough reason to want to be with a woman."

She shook her head. "You are an oddity."

He laughed.

"And what is so amusing?"

"You, calling me an oddity." The dark purple of her dress was accentuated by wild and mismatched orange and green embroidery. A wide band of ribbon at her waist repeated the orange. She wore an oddly shaped brown bonnet.

"Excellent point. Perhaps this is why we are friends?"

"Perhaps."

They walked through the art exhibits. And after about one minute, she sighed.

"What is it?"

"These paintings. Can we not look at something besides someone's face. Portrait after portrait. Who does that, anyway? Commissions a person to paint their face?" Hers looked pained for a moment.

"From the looks of things, everyone does that." He stopped in front of one. "Though perhaps some should not." The woman looked supremely unhappy. Her dog looked unhappy, and he imagined the person painting the image was unhappy as well. But Lady Evaline was not as amused as he expected her to be by him comments. "Come. You probably have a portrait. Everyone of title seems to get them done."

She shook her head. "I do not. As you said, some should not." She looked away.

He was astounded, his feet glued to the floor. After she took a step and he didn't follow, she turned. "Oh come now. I'd like to see more than just the portrait exhibit."

"But Lady Everly, surely you do not think you are one who should not get a portrait."

She waved her hand as if the conversation were unimportant, but he had seen the hurt in her eyes, and for some reason he did not want to let this go. "You are an only child for one."

She turned to him. "But even so, perhaps I'd like to be remembered for something besides my face."

He pondered her comments through the next two exhibits, being appropriately awed by one thing after another but puzzled still by her thoughts. Until they were coming upon the time for them to leave. "You know you have a lovely face."

She shook her head. "I know no such thing."

"How could you not?" Did she not look in the mirror every morning? Did she not see the beautiful color in her eyes? The set of her nose, the way her mouth sat just right, how full it was?

She turned to him. "Why are we still talking about this?"

"I think you need a portrait."

"And I disagree."

"But you're lovely. No one in the room was as lovely as your portrait is bound to be and they all have one."

Her eyes grew wider and she just stared for a moment. Something crossed her face for a moment, perhaps wonder. But then she just shook her head. "Be careful. Some would call you besotted."

Frustrated he led her out to their carriage. Why did this matter to him? He didn't know, but he said no more about it.

After their museum tour, he called at her house during calling hours and her father asked him into his study.

After the door was shut and they were both seated, Lord Hollings nodded at his brandy at the sideboard. "Help yourself Easton."

"No thank you. It's still early yet for me."

"Good man." He sipped his own drink then leaned forward. "It's not a secret you've been paying attention to my Evaline."

"Paying attention?"

"Don't try to hedge around about it. You've given impressions. Made promises."

He almost jumped to his feet. "I've made no promises.

And she and I are perfectly clear in our friendship." His alarm grew. What was her father trying to do here?

"So you are not coming to ask to court her?"

"I'm in no position to marry." They would be living on the poor blocks, or a tiny apartment in London. He had nothing.

"Why not?"

"I've nothing to support her with, no means, no estate…" He paused while Lord Hollings waved his arms around as though that were nothing.

"That doesn't matter one ilk if she fancies you."

"I don't think that she does." She couldn't fancy him, not with the way she was always putting him aside, telling him she refused to marry and what not.

Her father frowned. "People will talk. If there's nothing brewing between you then I need you to give her some space to find a gentleman who wants to move in that direction."

A strong disappointment rolled through him. She'd been his most enjoyable aspect of the Season this year. "I understand, my Lord."

Lord Hollings stood, and Oscar knew he was being dismissed. As he exited, he turned away from the front room where he could hear Lady Evaline's voice and instead walked out the front door.

Such a pity.

He walked to White's men's club. If Lady Evaline was no longer a possibility for entertainment, then he'd best see what the men had to offer. They took his coat as he walked in the door. Edward was across the room entertaining a group with something humorous enough they were laughing uproariously. Oscar turned the other direction. He joined a table of quieter gents and hoped for some good conversation. But they were deep into Whig ideology. He was fine with all the ideaologies. The man closest to him turned. "You, Easton. What do you think about enfranchising all of England?"

He looked from face to face and then shrugged. "I don't see a problem with expanding the vote to all landholders. Consider me, for example. I'm a second son. I have no land. So our vote is covered only by the Easton estate landholders?" The statement sat sourly in his belly and he wished it weren't true. And he wished he hadn't said it.

"Ah, but you'll have an estate soon enough. From what we hear, you've got that homely chit, the one who broke off her first engagement." He tapped his fingers trying to remember Lady Everly's name.

Oscar's emotions rose. The shock that he was being discussed in such a manner, the embarrassment in behalf of Lady Evaline, and the concern that perhaps he was ruining her chances at marriage...even though she seems uninclined.

"Lord Hollings' daughter."

Everyone at the table turned to him and Oscar decided that men were just as big of gossips as women.

He shook his head. "We have no understanding and I assure you I'm not heading in that direction."

"You'd be a fool not to. If she's the slightest tolerant of your company, you'd best continue that path."

"Check the books, man. We might need to adjust our bet."

Oscar stood. "Am I in the books?" He stepped toward the books. "If you'll excuse me." He dipped his head and hurried to check the infamous White's betting books.

As his finger moved down the ledger-like recordings, he saw bet after bet about his chances to win her heart. Some bet on how long it would take. Some bet on whether or not he would succeed. Most were betting against him. Some bet on whether or not it would be a love match. The next bet made his blood boil. Would he kiss her in the dark so as not to see her face. He ripped out the page. Was that it? Did the people of the ton find her unattractive? He thought back to their conversation about painting her portrait. They thought it, and she believed them. He shook his head, stared down the room of men who had all stopped what they were doing and watched him. He held up his fist with the torn page. "You call yourselves gentleman." Then he walked out of the room.

He spent the next week avoiding White's. He couldn't visit Lady Evaline. So he went to Jackson's boxing club and punched every one of the wealthy, entitled crummy men who thought themselves better than everyone, then at Tattersall's he went to look at horses, horses he couldn't buy. But nothing appealed quite as much as his time spent with Lady Evaline. And none of those activities mattered much to a man with very little funds. But her father was right. And especially after noting that they were a discussion in the books at Whites, if he wasn't going to marry her, then he best let her alone so that some man could. And he knew he wasn't truly besotted because he was fine with another man stepping in. Mostly fine. If the books were any indica-tion, most men did not respect her in the least. She at least deserved respect.

Weeks went by, and he went to fewer balls and fewer dinner parties. His brother made comments about at least making an effort. He started reading books on law, and then books on how to be a clergy. He'd all but decided to go back to university.

Today, he had no real desire to leave his office. He

shuffled through the papers on his desk, going through his correspondence. He did not know what to make of two letters that sat opened on his desk. One, an invitation from a man he didn't know, Mr. Shaw, to his house party in the tiny village of Charing Brook. The other, a letter from Lady Evaline, most curious and ridiculous in nature, asking if he would attend the very house party to which he was invited in Charing Brook. He shook his head, speaking to the air, "Of all the odd things to happen to a man." She'd signed it jointly with her aunt. He shook his head again. What woman invited other men of her acquaintance to attend house parties of people they didn't know? Though he should not have been surprised at the oddity. The lady herself was as odd as her letter. Her clothing, her mannerisms, her single status as the daughter of a Marquess. She was undoubtedly the most peculiar woman of his acquaintance. And she dressed as though choosing her miss-matched color patterns in the dark. And of course, he had been warned away by her own father. He snorted and then tossed both letters in with the other rubbish.

Several hours later, in the study playing pool, Oscar tried to tune out his brother. He had mentioned almost every woman of their acquaintance in some effort to encourage Oscar in a pursuit of her. Did the man exert himself with any other topic?

"If you will not try to court Lady Evaline, consider Lady Hetting."

Oscar choked. "*You* consider Lady Hetting." The woman seemed angry most of the time.

"She's got a fair dowry. One could live comfortably, the children as well, for many generations."

"It just doesn't sit well." Oscar knocked another ball in.

"To woo a woman, court her, marry her with the sole desire to earn her wealth."

"Then what of Miss Charlotte, Miss Catherine, or Miss Mary?" Edward waved his arms about in an odd exasperated manner. "You might woo, court and marry them for any number of non-monetary reasons and still have something to live off of while you're at it."

Oscar circled their billiard table, determined to end the game as quickly as possible now that the topic of conversation had so deteriorated. "You sound like an old matron, one of those marms trying to marry off her daughters." Oscar turned to him. "And instead of talking at me until I'm deaf from the sound, perhaps you could take a bit of your own advice." Oscar knocked a ball in, almost winning their game of pool. The sooner the better, in his mind.

Edward downed the rest of his brandy in one gulp. "I have no prospects as yet. And no money either while I've got you on my purse strings."

"Ah, feeling a bit possessive with Father's money, are you?"

Edward sighed loudly. This brought the twinge of guilt needed to soften Oscar's feelings about his brother's intrusive behavior. Edward's face was drawn, his eyes showed his concern as he tried to knock a ball in any pocket but missed terribly. "I don't understand how you can be so averse to marrying a woman for her money, averse to living off the charity of others, and yet have no qualms about living off of mine."

Attempting to hold on to the strings of good will Oscar still felt for his brother, he moved to stand beside him and placed a hand on his shoulder. "In matters of marriage a woman's heart is involved."

Edward shook his head as if he'd forgotten all about

their own struggles when their sister Tabitha was on the marriage mart. Oscar sighed. "Edward. I shall try not to be such a burden to you." He applied pressure to his shoulder, which was as much of an embrace as Oscar ever gave his brother, handed him the billiards stick, and turned from the room.

"Wait, where are you going?"

He glanced back over his shoulder. "I think I'll go house partying for a time, live off of other's kindness and offer my charm in return." He mock bowed and then made his way down the hall. He was joking in a way, but nothing could make him choose to stay with Edward one more day. Their sister Tabitha and her husband were coming to Edward's home for a visit over the Christmas holidays, but the last ten minutes of this conversation convinced Oscar he wished to be anywhere else but here.

He thought of Tabitha's two growing boys and smiled. He would miss the lads. Perhaps he could return early enough, by Twelfth Night, to see everyone. He thought of Edward's pressing ways. Or perhaps not.

His valet seemed to have guessed his plans. He had the trunks out already.

"Very good, Reed. Let's bring as much as possible in these trunks. I won't be returning to Edward's home for a time." He took off his jacket and placed it on the bed. *Edward's home.* Even though the rest of them had grown up in it, his oldest brother seemed more than anxious to kick them all from the premises. "We'll be attending as many house parties as we can find."

"Ah, so the usual. Sporting hunting wear and the finer dinner and ball attire."

"Yes, and more of the hunting. I know I shall have to dance attendance upon the ladies to earn my keep, but the

24

hunting serves a purpose as well, doesn't it?" He didn't expect Reed to answer, and the good valet knew it.

Oscar dug the now fortuitous letter out of the rubbish bin and left his man to the preparations. His feet hurried down to the kitchens almost of their own volition. His heart started to feel lighter the closer he moved to the one person he was truly loathe to leave. As soon as he stepped into the warm and cheery space, Mrs. Channing held out her hands, covered in flour though they were. "Is that my Oscar boy?" Her eyes crinkled with many years of smiling the same greeting to him.

"And how are you this afternoon?" He leaned closer for her customary kiss on his cheek. Then he squeezed her hands.

She studied his face and placed a hand at his cheek. "What is it? You've come in the middle of the afternoon with no smells of chocolate drifting anywhere."

"Do you think I come to you only to fill my unrelenting hunger?"

She nodded. "And to ease some of what troubles you."

"Which is far more important." He pulled out a chair. "I need a bit of the wisdom that always seems to come along with the delicious pastries."

She sat in the chair he indicated, and he pulled another up close. "I've received a letter."

"It must be an important one if you're here to talk to me about it."

"From a lady."

"Oh?" Her eyes sparkled with hope, but he didn't begrudge her desires to see him married. Unlike Edward, she wasn't anxious to be rid of him, only anxious to see him happy.

"Yes, it is most curious. She says she is writing with her

aunt at her side. They've both signed it. And wishes most urgently for me to attend a house party for her great-uncle in Charing Brook."

"And why does she most urgently need your attendance?"

"That's what I cannot fathom. She's not specific as to her reasons. Just that she thought I'd like to know, and she'd most dearly like my company."

Mrs. Channing's sweet eyes wrinkled in the confusion that Oscar himself also felt. "Who is this lady?"

Oscar chuckled to himself, at which Mrs. Channing looked up in surprise.

When he realized she must think he admired the young lady, he waved his hands. "No, nothing like that." He pulled the letter out of his pocket. "She's the most singular woman I've ever met. Obviously bold beyond belief, but it's more than that. She's delightfully unrestrained. And the best part about her, or so I thought, is that the woman has zero interest in marrying."

Mrs. Channing's expression turned wary. "We don't want to be entertaining those kinds of women. You were taught better, Mr. Oscar. And don't we both know it."

He stared at her for a moment, lost as to the reason for her sudden chastisement. And then he laid the letter out in front of her. "No, dear Mrs. Channing. You know me better than to think I would entertain those kinds of relationships. No. This woman is a lady. She's highly respectable. Perhaps her father being a Marquess contributes to her respectability, but she could never behave in the manner you misunderstood."

Mrs. Channing's face showed such an array of relief that Oscar added. "Nor would I. As you said, I was raised better. Come, let's read it together. Tell me what you make of it."

She patted his arm. "Too true. Forgive me. But a woman can never be too careful when it comes to the upbringing of the boys in her care."

Oscar smiled. Their cook really felt as though she'd partly raised him and each of his brothers and sister, and truth be told, she had.

"So why is she inviting you to attend this house party?" She held the paper out further from her face so she could see it and began to read aloud.

"Dear Mr. Oscar Easton:

I hope you will forgive my aunt's and my correspondence." Mrs. Channing paused. "See, there, at least she knows to include her aunt. I feel you are correct. She is a good moral woman at least."

He shook his head. "Continue."

She lifted the paper again. "We hope that you are in good health, etc. etc." She skipped ahead. "I am certain this letter may come as a bit of a surprise, but I find I need a favor. I will be attending a house party over Christmas and would greatly value your company as a friend, an associate. I find I might be alone much in this crowd and would like someone at my side who has no further expectations." Mrs. Channing frowned. "Now what can she mean by that?"

"You should see the way she dresses; this woman has oddity written all over her." He grinned. "Which I've always found intriguing. She's fascinating, really. Lady Evaline." The name felt like honey on his tongue. It fit her.

Mrs. Channing looked at him a little too closely at that, so he cleared his throat and pointed back to the letter. "I don't know what she means by any of it, and I had originally thrown it to the rubbish. Several days following, I received this invitation from the host himself, obviously as a result of her adding me to the guest list. I don't know him. I've never even heard of the man." He flipped the page back to her letter. "Here is the most interesting part of the whole thing. 'Dear Uncle Shaw will be choosing his heir one of these days, and only then will I feel comfortable around all the many who clamor for his attention.'"

Mrs. Channing frowned. "Do you think she writes hoping for protection? *Feel comfortable*, she says. How?" She shook her head and clucked her tongue. "I might steer clear of that whole mess if I were you. It sounds like a disaster waiting to happen... a whole family of people each hoping to be the man's heir? And how's he going to decide?" She shook her head. "This is exactly why people should just give their inheritance to the eldest son and be done with it."

Oscar ground his teeth, feeling not at all in agreement with Mrs. Channing's—and most of England's—manner of handling inheritances.

"I don't know. It sounds rather exciting to me, and since I'll be needing to find other opportunities in which to support myself soon, since I need to live elsewhere, I felt it best to take this eccentric uncle and his even more eccentric grandniece's offer and spend Christmas and possibly Twelfth Night with them."

"Oh, but Mr. Easton. Everyone will be coming home, even the lads. You wouldn't miss that, would you?"

"I will return before they leave. I'll just be missing most of it, which I think will suit us all just fine."

She pressed her lips together, but as always, kept her peace when she knew the conversation was over. "Would you like a basket for your journey?"

He nodded. "Thank you. I would like nothing more. And you can count on good diverting tales when I return."

He kissed her cheek. And his heart ached a little. Christmas without Mrs. Channing would seem very lonely indeed. But Christmas with Edward would be unbearable. "I'll be leaving at first light."

Chapter Three

Eva studied her reflection in her mirror. "Remy. I think I need the patch."

"Which one, my lady?" Remy held open a case of carefully created skin patches.

"This one, the pink."

Remy was past pointing out when things didn't match, but her nose did pinch just a bit, right at the end. It sort of wiggled, and her loyal servant pressed her lips together. Eva knew her maid wouldn't say anything, but she loved tempting her to do so. Eva mentally counted to five and then shook her head. "No. It doesn't match well, does it?"

Remy had the patience of all the ages combined. "I never know, my lady."

"I'm simply teasing you."

"Yes, my lady."

"Come, Remy." She held the case out. "I need to wear one. No one else will be wearing patches, and that means it is up to me. But pink is a bit garish, particularly with this orange color."

"Indeed."

"How about black. This patch here, a black dot right at my cheek below my eye."

Remy placed it with a bit of glue. Eva turned her head this way and that. "I think that's it." She studied the whole view. "I rather like this presentation. We shall make a large splash of ourselves, won't we?"

"You will, my lady, to be sure."

"Come, Remy. I keep you on because you are the absolute best. Am I that tiresome?"

"Not at all, my lady." Her face stoic, a mask really, refused to show emotion. She was the butler of all lady's maids, but Eva liked her rather reserved personality. She couldn't bear a giggling, intrusive woman at her side for so many hours. And she couldn't abide a simpering agreeable sort, either. She and Remy worked things very well together, and even though she said so little, Eva could read her reasonably well by the set of her mouth. And her nose.

"Well, we had best be off, or rather I had best. Have we heard back from that Mr. Easton yet?"

"No."

"When must I travel to the party of dear Mr. Shaw?"

"At first light, my lady."

She nodded. "Then I must have a bath tonight. We will want all of this out of my hair to travel, especially the powder... well, and the feathers. We can start with a fresh palette for the party. Please pack a trunk for yourself as well. Include all our normal necessaries and a few particulars for Christmas besides."

"Yes, my lady."

Eva arose, her hair towering tall on her head. At least she hadn't tried to conceal things deep inside for height. The styles of the past were more creative with hair. They towered above in all manner of ingenuity, but she had turbans and feathers at her disposal still. Let that Whims and Fancies column get wind of her styles and creations. Then they'd really have something to talk about. Not that Eva sought more attention. She rather hoped to eschew certain kinds.

Her father waited for her in the front hall. They would be going together to the opera. The perfect evening to dress with a bit more garish display than usual. Her father, long past commenting on her dress or hair, glanced briefly from her slippers to the top of her tallest feather and merely held out a hand. "Shall we?"

"Yes, thank you. I've been longing to see *Adelina*. I hope it is as good as people say."

"I suspect it isn't. Do they ever *watch* the opera? Really?"

He made a fair point. "I suppose it is more of a see-and-be-seen type of activity."

His eyes travelled her whole presentation again and then nodded. "Indeed."

Fair point. Her garish appearance only confirmed her statement, certainly.

"But I do really long to see it. And I suspect I shall cry."

He didn't respond. She didn't expect him to. When they sat together in the carriage, she braved the strongest thought that seemed to encompass them both. "It was Mother's favorite."

His face pinched a moment and then cleared. When his gaze met hers, his eyes were full of feeling. Which kind of feeling she could not even guess, but feeling nonetheless. She held her breath.

He nodded. "Yes, it was." He patted her hand. "We shall think on her and remember all she's done for us."

Eva nodded, her throat thick and sharp as she tried to swallow.

It had been a year now. Eva's mother had only seen one Season, her daughter's coming out. And then she was taken abruptly and completely by the evil and mysterious fevers. The doctor said it could be any number of illnesses, but to simplify, it was covered by the web of darkness called "fevers."

Eva had been taken away immediately out of the home for her protection. By the time she was allowed to return, her mother had been long gone from the earth and the house scoured of her presence.

Eva's year of mourning had been one long confusing picture filled with advice and friendship from every possible front. When she folded the last of her black and grey clothing away in her trunk full of her most precious things, she could no longer tell who of all the friends were sincere. She hadn't the slightest idea who wanted anything more to do with her other than a possible alignment with their son or perhaps a match with her father. It seemed people wanted a connection with her only for some reason totally and wholly unrelated to her as a person.

She also found it difficult to find an advisor after her mother's passing. Her father had asked his sister, Lady Wither, to chaperone and sponsor her activities for a subsequent Season, but Eva found that she and her aunt differed on most things. Eva had created ways to irritate and embarrass her aunt, but not out of spite. It was more a form of independence. She was not finished mourning; no matter how much time had passed, she was not finished. She did not want a husband. She was tired of typical activities that a Season would include and she was not allowed to choose her acquaintances.

So she chose to be eccentric; she could choose her hair-styles. She could embellish and change her dresses that were commissioned by her aunt. She would have her own style if it was the one thing granted to her. At last, her aunt gave up; her father stopped discussing it, and she was left to herself and her own social decisions. Which was precisely what she most wanted. There was also the matter of hoping to never marry. That subject had yet to be retired.

The invitation to Uncle Shaw's house party had been an exception to her hope to not socialize much. Her father had absolutely insisted, upon threats of losing all pin money, that she attend and be good to her uncle.

She adored the sweet man. She had no trouble at all doting on him. But attend a house party? With strangers? Enduring their stares, feeling their disdain. The ostracizing, especially after her broken engagement, used to needle at her of course, but over time, her loneliness had grown and she almost feared social gatherings without a friend.

She'd done the only thing she could think of to do: Invite a man she didn't know well but knew him to be the last man interested in marrying her or anyone. Oscar Easton would never get the wrong idea about her. He had not even blinked about any of her eccentric tastes. He seemed to take it in stride, perhaps even respect her choices as her own. Either that or he cared very little. She laughed, thinking about her audacity in writing him. But hopefully he would be intrigued enough to come. She'd have at least one person she knew to be a friend at this party besides her uncle. Perhaps he would be an ally if needed.

Her father looked out of their carriage window. "It is unseasonably cold. Will you be warm enough?"

Her feet shifted on the warm blocks. "I will. We shall

hurry in so as not to linger in the cold, and then they keep our boxes warm."

He nodded. "That they do. And I've instructed Jacques to pull up to the very front."

"Thank you."

They were escorted to the front though many chose to stop further out and walk on the frozen ground. Their footman opened the door. Her father descended, turned, and held out his hand.

She placed her hand on his arm. "You are so thoughtful. Thank you, Father."

"It is a pleasure to take care of you, my sweet. I will miss you during Christmas. Thank you for supporting Mr. Shaw."

She sucked in a breath. He hadn't called her anything remotely endearing in many years.

"I won't always be here, you know. I had hoped to know of your future long before now."

"Yes, I know, Father. But I can't see how there's a single worry. I will have means the whole of my life. I can afford to be single or married as I so choose. I am well."

"I would like to pass the estate and title along to someone in our line. To your son, if you are so blessed."

Her heart ached with a sharp twinge. "Yes." But she looked away, fighting the guilt and responsibility that descended on her shoulders as it always did when she thought of the estate, of the Marquisette of her father. Already, he was managing their affairs long past many of his age who had begun to hand things over to their sons. A son he never had.

She sighed. "I'm sorry, Father. I have been selfish. Perhaps I will attempt to find a good father to your heir."

He bristled a bit, and she regretted her cynical sounding words.

"That is not what I most concern myself over. As I said, I long to see you settled, cared for, loved. You can pay all the servants in the world to see after your needs, but I want more for you."

She nodded slowly.

"Let us speak no more of it."

As they made their way into the grand Opera Hall, she felt everyone's gaze. Instead of the thrill she expected, she now felt a bit ridiculous at her fashion choice. Her father's words had sent such a powerful reminder of her expected purpose in life that she couldn't enjoy her outward rebellion. What was the fun of a brightly colored orange gown with purple embroidery and this towering feathered turban, if she could not flaunt it and enjoy the reactions of others?

The next morning she was on her way. Her father had not seen her off. As she searched the front facing windows of her home, she thought she saw movement. That was to be all the farewell she received.

Remy, as stoic as ever, read a book in her quiet corner of the carriage. Mrs. Widget, her chaperone of sorts, another aunt on her father's side, dozed in the other corner and for a moment, sadness pinched Eva's chest. Was this to be her lot? Company in companions and servants? A feeling of great restlessness overtook her, and she rapped on the ceiling.

A hatch opened and her coachman's face appeared.

"Push the horses. I wish for us to arrive in record time."

"Yes, my lady." He closed the hatch.

The resulting jolt forward was satisfying, but it did not wipe away her discontent. With a sigh, she leaned back against her seat and tried to block out her thoughts, but they came crowding in anyway, as thoughts do. Former fiancé, mean women in the ton, gentlemen who thought it fair to ridicule, people seeking her wealth, a father who couldn't say goodbye, a mother she longed to see. Every available space in her thoughts was filled until she muttered, "Enough." She reached in her bag and pulled out a new project. Her embroidery thread sat in a pile at her side and she began work on the gloves. She was adding Christmas touches to her white gloves, a line of holly with red berries, woven from the back of her hand all the way up her arm. She was nearly finished with her fourth pair. As she worked, the concentration did the trick and she was free of the worst of her concerns...for a time.

Chapter Four

Oscar's cravat was less restrictive the farther away from his family estate he traveled. He would miss his siblings—Tabitha, even Edward. But his short visit at the end of the holiday would have to suffice. With any luck, he could be back by Twelfth Night. That would appease Tabitha. If he planned things just right, he'd have two days home—*correction*—Edward's home, as he acted as though it were already his, and then Oscar would be off to another party for which he'd received an invitation. The men were some of his Corinthian friends. They had planned a phaeton race that got some attention in the ton. Oscar needed to do some work on his phaeton in order to make it faster, but he was low on funds. He would have to wait a couple months to save his allowance. It galled him to no end. Edward no doubt had access to any funds he desired. Such liberty was wasted on a man who never did anything.

There had to be another way to function in this world, a way that didn't involve begging his family's money off his brother. Oscar was curious about Mr. Shaw. The man had made himself a considerable fortune. He'd grown a respectable estate to a huge merchant empire. Perhaps Oscar would have a moment to talk with the man. There might be other ways for Oscar to earn his own way, ways that did not include marrying a girl for her dowry or getting commissioned in the military.

He hadn't given himself enough time to respond to Lady Evaline. At any rate, he felt odd doing so. He'd never corresponded with a woman before, especially not a woman and her aunt jointly. He doubted very much that the woman's aunt was a part of any letter at all, but he had to hand it to Lady Evaline. She was aware of Society's rules and was creative enough to seemingly abide by them. Now, to see just exactly what she had up her, no doubt rather outlandish, sleeves.

As the hours dragged on one long minute at a time, he admitted he wouldn't be making this journey at all if it weren't for Edward. He'd actually like to stay at his childhood home, eat Mrs. Channing's food, play with his nephews… Oscar frowned at no one in particular. His valet had fallen asleep hours ago. The countryside, innocent though it was, received the brunt of his frustration. And suddenly he could bear the inside of his carriage no longer. He rapped on the roof. "Jacques!"

The carriage slowed. And before it even came to a full stop, Oscar hopped out.

"Whoa!" A man's shout behind him, too close, jerked Oscar's attention to the bend in the trees. A carriage with a set of four horses came tearing around the bend toward them. "Whoa!" The driver stood, pulling on the reins, but the team of horses was moving way too quickly. They were bound to hit Oscar's carriage. "Jump aside!" he shouted as he jumped back. His driver started the horses, who leapt ahead at the whip on their backs. Jacques expertly moved the carriage to the side of the road quickly enough that the other carriage came careening to a stop right beside them instead of barreling into the back of them.

If Oscar hadn't already been frustrated and bored and downright angry at his brother, he might not have stomped so furiously toward the other carriage, but as things were, his feet had led him there and he now stared up at the driver. "What in the blazes! Are you out of your mind? Who drives at those speeds on these roads?"

The driver dipped his head almost as if he agreed with Oscar, and then the door opened. "We do." The feathers in her hair and the bright colored travelling clothes should have clued him in immediately, but he blinked twice at a woman standing before him when he expected a man. "Lady Evaline?"

"Mr. Easton." She dipped a quick half curtsey, as though she didn't make a habit of curtseys, which she might not as far as he knew. She had her own manner of doing so many other things.

"You instructed your driver to go at those speeds on these roads?" He was incredulous. He peered around her to see who else might have done such a thing.

"It is only I, my maid, and my chaperone Aunt, a Mrs. Widget, if you are that intrigued. She's hard of hearing and likely still asleep."

His mouth twitched. "You have a chaperone named Mrs. Widget?"

"Yes, and she's the perfect kind, so I wouldn't be too overly dismissive of someone because of a name."

"The perfect kind? As in hard of hearing and sleeps

through most things?" He tried to stifle a sudden desire to laugh.

"Precisely." One long feather fell forward and was on its way to tickling her nose. He watched it hovering about, drooping further, almost down in front of her face.

"Is this the same Aunt from whom I recently received correspondence of the most unique kind?"

Her slight blush intrigued him. He'd previously thought her beyond ever feeling embarrassment.

"Her sister." She offered no further explanation.

She wore bright yellow again, as she had the first day they'd met. One day he would ask her why she was so prone to the ridiculous in her manner of dress, but that day was not today. He stood taller. "You could have killed your horses just now and destroyed my carriage."

"Who stops in the middle of the road just after a bend?" She crossed her arms. "If an accident hadn't been avoided, I'd dare say it would be half your fault as well as mine."

"We stopped far enough along after the bend that anyone going a *normal safe speed* could have stopped without problem."

"And yet, we stopped, without problem." She raised an eyebrow in challenge, and he was torn between laughing and frowning. The feather flipped back up in the air with the toss of her head. "And now, as you must discern for yourself, we are wasting our daylight hours." She waved her hand. "George. Let's be off." She curtseyed to Oscar, low, deep, and probably mockingly, then she made her way to her carriage door.

She turned back and called over her shoulder. "Mr. Easton. Thank you for coming to my uncle's house party."

He dipped his head, not sure what to say to that. But

then he ran to his own carriage. "Jacques, we are off!" As soon as he was close enough, he winked. "Best if we beat this lady to it."

"Very good, sir." The horses jerked ahead before Oscar had even closed the door. He leaned out and saluted an open-mouthed Lady Evaline and they continued on to Charing Brook in Westmoreland at a reasonable, quick, but safe speed. She would not be able to pull ahead of his large equipage. He enjoyed every minute imagining her fuming in her own carriage. It served her right for nearly running him down.

What an interesting woman. As maddening as their interactions just now, he had to laugh. This house party would be nothing if not intriguing. And the stories he could tell. He spent the remainder of their journey congratulating himself for deciding to attend the party, and for his carriage's position in first place. Then he laughed aloud as he tried to predict her expression were she to see his smug smile.

But as they were about to arrive, the entrance to her uncle's front drive widened, and Lady Evaline's horses thundered past him, nearly clipping his carriage. She slowed just enough to appear respectable before stopping in front of the home.

"Of all the reckless, ridiculous, risky things to do," he grumbled, hating that she forced him into the role as some old ninny, complaining about fast carriages. But she was a class all by herself if she would tear into the front drive of a home like that. She stepped down, her hand in that of a footman. An older matronly-looking woman, dressed as blandly as Lady Evaline was garish, stepped out behind her. She curtseyed deeply and then kissed an older gentleman on the cheek. Must be Mr. Shaw. He led her into the house with a hand on his arm. Mrs. Widget followed behind. Servants unloaded five trunks. Five. Her lady's maid seemed to hover about the process, making certain things were just right. And then the whole entourage entered the home.

"What does a woman need five trunks for, Reed?"

"They have many more accessories than we, but that does seem excessive."

"Yes."

When her carriage moved along, Oscar approached with their own. Mr. Shaw did not come to their carriage door to greet them, but the butler and housekeeper smiled warmly.

"Welcome to Ivy Manor."

The home towered above him in a pleasant way. The stone aged but beautiful. The face of a boy moved and then disappeared from an upper window. "Thank you. I am Mr. Oscar Easton."

"Ah, yes, Mr. Easton. Mr. Shaw is expecting you. We will show you to your rooms." The butler nodded to him and Reed. "You may refresh yourself and then Mr. Shaw will see you in the front parlor when you are ready. Dinner will be late tonight or of course, you may request a tray."

"Thank you." Oscar shrugged more comfortably into his jacket and stretched his neck from one side to another. Time to enjoy himself, be an engaging guest, and spend the holidays far from Edward and his constant reminders that Oscar was leeching off the family coffers.

As soon as he was upstairs, he changed his shirt, splashed water on his face and asked Reed to redo his cravat. Then he left his capable valet to unpack while Oscar went in search of his host.

The servants directed him to the front receiving room

where the focus of his and everyone in the room's immediate attention was drawn to Lady Evaline.

She sat next to Mr. Shaw as though on a throne of her own. Or did it just appear to Oscar that way? Her yellow dress shone as if from the sun itself. Mr. Shaw and four others surrounded her, listening to every word. After a moment, the room burst into laughter. Oscar smiled. Despite his slight irritation from earlier, he was pleased she could be such a success considering how lonely she'd expected to be. Her aunt sat in the corner, eyes closed. Oscar shook his head. That woman would serve no purpose.

The footman announced him. "Mr. Oscar Easton."

Everyone stood and curtseyed or bowed. Lady Evaline last of all. Their eyes met, and he felt something odd that rumbled in his chest. She murmured something to Mr. Shaw who held out his hand. "Come, Mr. Easton. Welcome to my home and to our party."

"Thank you. I look forward to spending Christmas with all of you." He looked around at the small group gathered and then took the seat next to Mr. Shaw. "I've heard only the best of things."

"About you as well. You seem to have gained a loyal friend in Lady Evaline here."

"I am pleased to hear it. She's quite a strong ally of yours."

"Then we are doubly blessed." His eyes sparkled kindly at Lady Evaline. Oscar was struck by the close rapport between them. How had such a thing come to be? With one's great-uncle?

"Tell me about your position in the family." Mr. Shaw turned an open and interested expression toward Oscar.

"I'm the second eldest. The Easton Estate rests in my brother Edward's capable hands."

"Ah yes. And nothing in yours?"

"Not particularly, no."

"Inheritances are a big topic here amongst us in this family. I think you will find many sympathetic ears in regards to being the one who doesn't inherit."

Everyone in their small group seemed to lean closer. The tension increased enough that Oscar wondered if he might feel it stretch to its breaking point. And then Evaline laughed, a loud tinkling sound. "But dear Mr. Easton doesn't have a care in the world about that."

"He might want to care about a hefty exchange of money. Everyone should care about that. Have you considered investing, lad?"

Oscar hadn't been called lad in over two decades, but he perked up in great interest and leaned closer so that he might speak without others hearing. "I have. I hope during our time together to be able to learn more from you about how to move about in Society in my situation, to better my financial status and to perhaps not have to rely so heavily on others." He leaned ever closer to express the last bits, but Evaline had leaned closer as well.

Confound the woman. Did she have no cares for a man's personal business?

"Naturally. I am at your disposal." Mr. Shaw nodded.

Did Oscar imagine it or was Lady Evaline overly pleased?

Chapter Five

Eva was secretly happy that Mr. Easton might have some benefit to attending this house party with her. What kind of man was so gallant as to accept such an eccentric invitation? Either the good hearted or the bored. She suspected he might be a bit of both. But surely he was not in need of funds? Men in need of funds concerned her. Was she wise in inviting him to the party?

Perhaps he could learn something from Mr. Shaw. Perhaps he could even find someone to marry. Though she knew this to be the very last idea in his handsome head, it would be good for him, at least she thought so. She studied the women in the room. None of them were looking too kindly in her direction, but not many usually did. She found during her return to another Season that she was a bit much for any person, but particularly another woman. She adjusted the angle of her head, enjoying the wiggling feather at the top of her hair she knew shook there. And certainly many remembered the scandal and with that in her wake, what could she do?

She turned to her guest. "Mr. Easton. Have you met everyone in our cozy group here?"

"I don't believe I have."

"We shall amend things this moment. We have arrived a bit ahead of most of the guests, but allow me to present Mr. and Mrs. Taylor. In her great magnanimous manner, Mrs. Taylor is assisting Mr. Shaw in hosting this very party."

"I'm pleased to meet you both." Oscar turned to Mr. Taylor. "Will you be participating in any sort of hunt while we are here?"

He glanced at his wife. "As a matter of fact, yes…"

Mrs. Taylor shook her head and cut her husband off. "No, of course not. I'm terribly sorry, but you will notice there just isn't anything left out there in these cold parts to hunt."

"Perhaps some grouse, a partridge, a stray deer?" Mr. Taylor looked almost as if he might beg for a bone from his wife.

She merely sniffed, and Eva knew that Oscar would be talking to Mr. Taylor later without the presence of Mrs. Taylor.

Eva continued. "And I have just recently met Lady Constance Riley who, happenstance, is my cousin. If you can believe, we have never met—nor did I know of her, until now. But pleased I am to have more family." She waved her hand. "And this is Miss Darlene Evans."

Oscar nodded to both. They seemed remarkably lovely. Well presented. He smiled at Miss Darlene who was the nearest to him of the two. "I wonder if I might interest you in a walk about the grounds tomorrow?"

Eva shook her head and none too subtly. She couldn't help herself. The idea that Mr. Easton would take a walk on the grounds with someone other than she herself suddenly seemed absurd. Though she'd just hoped for a bit of happiness in regards to marriage for him, now did not seem the time to be walking the grounds without Eva. What if she lost her friendship to Mr. Easton because he suddenly became enamored with one of these women? Eva nodded in their direction. "Mr. Easton is my particular friend. I believe we shall *all* be taking a walk about the grounds. The Taylor's have promised a tour. Isn't that correct, Mrs. Taylor?"

"It certainly is." Mrs. Taylor then carried on about the house party's many activities for a long enough moment that Eva began to feel remorse. Why had she behaved in such a manner? Her eyes met Mr. Easton's, which were full of questions.

"Of course. We can all go together. I'm certain we hope to make new friends while we are here." Oscar smiled at Miss Darlene, who was friendly but glanced twice in Lady Evaline's direction before staring at her hands.

Mr. Easton cleared his throat. "I wonder, Lady Evaline, if you might take a turn with me?"

"Feeling restless, are you?" She tittered about in her seat, fanned her face and then when his attention did not waver, she tucked her fan away. "Oh, very well. If you'll excuse me." She smiled at Mr. Shaw.

"Of course, my dear. I shall see you at dinner."

As soon as Lady Evaline stood, Mrs. Taylor took her seat.

Oscar and Eva walked sedately to the opposite side of the room and then she hissed in his ear. "What couldn't wait?"

"Just wondering about what you said back there? Am I your particular friend? We will all go together?"

"You don't know what it means to be someone's particular friend?"

"Lady Evaline …. of all the ridiculous, half-baked ideas. I don't know specifically what idea, but would you have everyone think we are betrothed? I must know at once your plans."

"Oh, fine. I need us to be particular friends and for you to escort me to most things for the first couple days and then you can get to know whichever of the other ladies you would like. While still being my friend."

"I don't have a real need to get to know anyone else. I thought it would be a good, helpful thing to do for our hosts. That's what you do at a house party, entertain each other. Miss Darlene seemed lovely…"

She stared at him with both eyebrows raised.

"And she was a pretty woman. I wouldn't mind getting to know her."

Eva retorted, "I thought you were the furthest thing from marriage of anyone I know."

"I am… wait, what? Why would you say such a thing?"

"From what you've said. Everyone knows Mr. Oscar Easton is not looking for anything serious with anyone."

He seemed to consider that for a moment. An uncomfortable feather tickled her insides. "You *are* far from desiring marriage, am I right?"

"Certainly." He turned the full force of his handsome gaze down into hers and she sucked in a breath. "Allow me to understand. You asked me to come because you knew I would not be here, attempting to marry myself off?"

"I asked you because I knew you would not be trying to marry yourself off… to me." She felt her face heat. "And that is what I need most right now, a man to… be at my side to scare off the others, and a friend when no one else seems interested in filling the position. Is that too much to ask? Will you wish you hadn't come in the first place?"

The perceptive eyes that tried to read her very soul stared long enough that she could almost feel the others at the party begin to wonder at just how intimately attached were she and Mr. Easton. But at last he nodded, once. "Plenty of conversations and walks to be had without marrying anyone."

"I won't stand in your way of any of that. I'm sorry, I reacted too quickly without thinking. Even a walk with Miss Darlene would be perfectly fine. I… I guess I would really like a friend. That's what I need." Her voice cracked, and the vulnerability she was showing to a relative stranger made her cringe.

"Of course." He glanced around the room. Most people looked in their direction every now and again. "I was your friend before I arrived. That part is easy." His new smile set her at ease and sent an array of lovely warmth through her.

"We're drawing attention. I suspect you don't want this much speculation surrounding the two of us?" His one eyebrow wiggled slightly. Just enough that Eva suspected it to be great fun to watch were he to truly descend into a great tease.

"You are quite correct. For your sake more than mine. My reputation has already suffered from mistaken attachment to another." She bit her tongue, not wanting to say more, not wanting to lay her whole past at his feet.

"Are you going to tell me what motivates your eccentric and intriguing mind?"

"Yes, tonight. We'll go for a walk after dinner, or if there are cards, we'll find a moment."

"Excellent, and now, shall we return to the others? I think we are neglecting the other guests."

"You care about neglecting the guests?" Was he the host now?

"I don't care terribly much, but it is my manner in which to be of service. I am here, enjoying their lovely rooms, their activities, all the meals. I wish to do something of use in return."

"Such a singular reaction." She studied him until he was obviously ready to leave her side.

"Why do you study me so? And singular? I? Am singular?" His gaze travelled over the whole of her, to the top of her feathers.

And she laughed. "Understood. Then so be it. Neither of us is singular."

"Or we both are."

They turned and made their way to sit at the fringe of the group.

"I've taken you from your throne." Mr. Easton's chin indicated her previous seat that was now occupied by an extraordinarily self-important Mrs. Taylor.

"Never fear, Mr. Easton. I shall reclaim it."

He murmured close into her ear so that his breath tickled her neck in a surprisingly pleasant manner. "Tell me something. Are you after his fortune?"

The face she whipped back to look into his own discovered his so near that their noses almost touched. But he didn't back away. A challenging light flickered in his eyes.

But she must quell this thought immediately. "No. I'm wealthy enough, thank you."

He studied her again and then seemed satisfied. With an accepting nod, he turned back to the group again. "So

JEN GEIGLE JOHNSON

part of our purpose here is not to ingratiate yourself to the wealthy host?"

"Certainly not."

She wished for a fan. He was fifty times more interesting than anyone else in the room. Goodness, she was going to have a time of it at this house party, a deliciously enjoyable time. And it had been far too long since she'd truly enjoyed herself. "Thank you for coming, Mr. Easton."

"My pleasure, Lady Evaline."

Chapter Six

That evening Oscar sat at a Whist table, waiting for a foursome to gather, but every stray gaze was captured by Evaline who sat at another. She wore the brightest green he'd seen in a gown. What made that woman act the way she did? At any rate, he'd have his work to do to keep her happy and to be a good guest. He wished to know Mr. Shaw better, which might prove a challenge with everyone here trying to monopolize all his time.

His thoughts were interrupted when Miss Darlene Evans arrived with a sweet smile. She sat across from Oscar, and they soon had their four. Her smiles dimmed as she proved to be a remarkably competitive player. She stared daggers at his cards. He couldn't quite guess what she wanted from him, but he placed his only card of the current suit down on the table. Her smile grew. Well, at least he'd pleased her. She adjusted her hand, then asked, "Tell me, how do you all know Mr. Shaw?"

The man at Oscar's right, a Mr. Talmus, adjusted his

cards as well before placing his suit. "Oh, you've opened a box with that question."

"She has?" Oscar looked from face to face at their table.

"Certainly." Mr. Talmus indicated each person at the table. "And now we're going to hear everyone's claim to the money."

"The money?" Miss Evans shook her head.

"Everyone is going to tell you how they are intimately connected to dear Mr. Shaw, how he did such and such and nonesuch and so much that even you will be convinced that they are the dear, lost relative and sure to inherit."

Oscar half nodded when Mr. Talmus' partner, a Lady Fenning, sniffed. "Well, some of us are in fact very dear to Mr. Shaw. He's said so himself."

"And here we go." Mr. Talmus sat back. "Let's hear. Just how dear to Mr. Shaw are you?"

"Come, man. No need to challenge the lady." Oscar hoped for a lighter tone. "Since I seem to be one of few who have no connection to him whatsoever, perhaps I'll share just how *little* I know him?" He nodded. "What is his business?"

Mr. Talmus thankfully stopped his inquisition and placed another card. "He's done well in shipping. He invested in a good fleet and then bought some of his own."

"He's brought me back the loveliest things from the East Indies." Lady Fenning lifted her arms. "This shawl was a gift."

Miss Evans and Oscar shared a gaze and Oscar was pleased to discover that he was not the only one who thought their table sounded a bit too mercenary.

"Tell me, Miss Evans, of your home."

Her smile grew. "That will be easy enough. I grew up right here in Charing Brook. My father was the vicar."

"Oh, excellent. Then I shall seek you out for all trips to town."

They played out the hand and three more before most were ready to call it a night, or switch up partners.

Mrs. Taylor stood on the other side of the room. "We are so pleased that Lady Evaline would play for us."

Oscar lifted his chin. "Ah." He stood and made his way closer to the piano.

She met his gaze. "Would you turn pages?"

He nodded. When they were seated, close enough that her lovely smells of violets and vanilla filled the air around them, she murmured, "I'm not very good." The quiver of her lip told him she was not in jest.

"Then you have two choices." He pretended to shuffle her papers.

"What are they?"

"Pretend you are quite good." The wink he gave her brought out a slight pink to her cheeks. He was so amazed by it, he forgot to continue.

"Or?"

He choked and cleared his throat. "Blame your playing on me. I'm abominably horrid at turning pages in time. And I nudge people while they play." He gently lifted his elbow. "See, who could be proficient with such as I at the bench?"

She laughed. And then pressed her lips together for a moment. "Seems I'll have to give a go at both my options then."

He eyed their audience. This house party would be interesting at minimum. So many people he would never expect to see in one room. A good group of lords and some he ran into at Whites now and again and others from the far reaches of Britain he had barely heard of before today.

Mr. Shaw had far reaching connections indeed. "They're an easy crowd. These ladies cannot be as proficient as you."

Her fingers began the first notes. "And now I shall feel intimidated. But your presence gives me courage. I'll tell you when to turn, or nudge me, or both." Her lips twitched, and Oscar found himself interested in the curve of her upper lip. It had a fascinating dip right in the center.

She cleared her throat. "Be ready."

"Yes." He lifted his fingers up to the page.

"Now."

He turned it, leaning across her, and then accidentally bumped the pages so they almost fell. He reached out with two hands to press the pages against the piano so they wouldn't fall to the floor. "Right, then."

She kept playing, remarkably, leaning around his arms so she could still see the notes. "You were not in jest."

"I was, actually." He cleared his throat. "Apologies."

"Hmm."

"I'm usually much more proficient." He kept his hand up on the piano, ready to turn again and this time not make a bumble of things.

"Here's the part where we sing."

"Wait, what?" His mouth went immediately dry.

"It's a duet. You do sing, don't you?"

"Not if I can help it." He stared into her face but of course she wasn't looking and missed the extreme sincerity in his expression.

"Come now. Turn."

He turned the page, and she started to sing. For a moment he quite forgot himself. She sang beautifully. The soft clear kind of voice that would never distract. He found himself carried away for a moment, paying close attention.

"Your turn."

He groaned. "I really don't…"

"Now." She pointed to his part and then kept playing.

"Of all the…" He started to sing. It was an interesting folk tune that had a simple section, his part, and he handled it moderately well. But wished to never do anything of the like again.

"Well done. You're better than I thought."

He didn't answer, just concentrated on turning the remaining few pages. When they were finished, he took a moment to recover. His heart beat unevenly and his hands… were they clammy? Was he a young nervous teen afraid of his first ball?

He pressed his lips together and bowed to the room as all applauded.

"You did excellently."

"And you've accomplished quite a feat."

"Oh? And what's that?"

"You have witnessed my first and last vocal performance."

"What a shame. You sang quite well."

"Hmm." He clasped his hands behind his back to hide their mild shaking.

They moved to find seats. He adjusted his several times before he was comfortable, but then only for a moment. "Forgive me." He dipped his head to Lady Evaline and moved to stand at the back of the room. A long soft exhale helped him re-center as he leaned back against the wall. What on earth had come over him? His family would ne'er believe he'd done such a thing. They were no doubt puzzled over this whole house party decision in the first place.

He studied the back of Lady Evaline's head. She'd left the feathers in her room, but the towering pile of curls was in keeping with what he was coming to see as her style. No other lady in the room had quite as elaborate a design on their heads. It suited her. But Oscar wondered if there was more to her style choices than simple eccentricity. She was nervous, scared even, to play and sing. Maybe she didn't crave attention like he'd originally assumed? Why try to stand out the way she did all the time?

He closed his eyes. Why was he even pondering this woman, or any woman's, fashion choices? The last thought he'd had about anyone's fashion besides his own had been a silly conversation with Tabitha about a new style of boot. He missed his sister.

Lady Evaline shifted in her seat. He stood up straighter, then relaxed when she merely continued to listen to the next person who was playing the piano. Was he at her beck and call? He turned and slipped from the room, uncomfortable with this feeling of... something... for her. Responsibility. He couldn't make his own feelings out. Never in his life had he been so accommodating of another. He would have been content all his life to never sing in front of another yet had sung in front of an entire audience because of her. People would think him addled or besotted and he could accept neither of those options.

Tomorrow, he would do what he wanted, when he wanted, and Lady Evaline could find her own way at this party.

Chapter Seven

Eva knew the minute Mr. Easton stepped out of the room. She had acquired a new awareness of him. But it was more than that. The room fizzled to a dull shade of grey without him in it. Curious. When had he become the most entertaining part of her existence?

Perhaps It was easy to see why he would be so. When she had no interest in marrying, the other men had little interest for her. And the women… perhaps she should strike up a friendship. She had a cousin, after all. She studied Lady Constance's profile. Her clothing was new, the latest fashion. She was open and generally pleased. Lady Constance was quite lovely.

Eva stood and moved to sit at her side. "Hello, cousin."

She startled. "Hello."

Their voices were hushed. Mr. Talmus had stood and was going to say something. What on earth could the grumpy man hope to say to the group?

He lifted his chin. "I have a recitation."

"My, oh my." Eva widened her eyes.

"What do you suppose a man such as he would recite?"

Mr. Talmus stood taller. "Wellington's charge, an ode to the man."

Lady Constance nodded, slowly. "Ah, yes."

As one, the two sunk lower in their seats. Eva pulled out her fan. "Would you care for a walk?"

"Yes, dare we leave in the middle?"

His voice rose, evidence of a particularly passionately felt passage.

"I don't know that we dare."

"Perhaps we could take a turn though, about the room?"

"And fall out the door?"

Eva bit back a giggle. Astounded at herself, giggling of all things, she nearly choked on her subsequent laugh. "Let us give an attempt."

They rose. Lady Constance took her arm, and they moved at a crawling pace about the back of the room. "Where has your friend gone?" Her question took Eva by surprise. "Friend?"

"Or perhaps he is more?" Lady Constance's daring twinkle gave Eva pause. "He?"

"A Mr. H?"

Eva opened her mouth in surprise. "Yes, my friend. Friend. And I don't know where he has gone? Is he gone?"

"Yes, he stepped out I believe. And hasn't returned." Her gaze flit to the door with the hint of a suggestion.

"I don't understand."

"Lady Evaline, he waits for you."

The laugh barreled out without Eva able to squelch it. "Oh dear no."

A couple from the back row glanced over their shoulders at the pair of them.

Eva shook her head again. "Not at all like that. We are friends, yes. But that's where it stops."

The skepticism all over Lady Constance's face and posture gave Eva pause. "Perhaps you wish to move forward with that understanding but his feelings, at least, are written plain as day on his face."

She started to laugh again but then stopped. "What do you mean?" A great wave of angst began to swell inside.

"Oh, Lady Evaline. Just to see you at the piano together. It was obvious to all. His face, his bearing, everything. It was the most precious thing I've ever seen. If you say you don't care for him in that way, I have no choice but to believe, but had you not said anything, I would have assumed you both the happiest couple, ready to read your banns. He is smitten indeed." She pressed her lips together as if she might say more but forbear.

Eva pressed her hand closer at her arm. "I must thank you for making me aware. Are you… quite certain?"

"Oh yes."

Eva sucked in a breath and grabbed her stomach a moment before calming her outward appearance. "This is not what I want."

"I don't know why not. He's perfectly handsome, and seems to dote on you. He's respectable…"

"As if that's all that matters." Her heart started flipping around in her chest like it didn't know what to do with itself. A part of her wanted to smile at the revelation, the other part wanted to run and hide and still another pounded in great dread. With a great flood, a surge of memories came back, of her first love, of his proposal, of her plans for happiness all her days and then the moment she saw him kissing another. She shook her head. "No."

"No?" Lady Constance started to laugh, but then stopped and studied her closer. "Are you well?"

"Yes, perfectly." She rested her hand against the wall. "But I think I need my room."

"Let's step into the hall. Certainly. We'll call for someone to escort you."

As soon as they were in the hall, Lady Constance called a servant and Eva was on her way up the stairs on the arm of a footman. She turned at her door. "Thank you. I'm fine now."

"Very good, my lady. I was told to remind you to please ring your bell for a tray. Cook has solutions for many ailments." He bowed and was down the hall and out of sight within a few moments.

She was about to enter her room, ready to fall on her bed and sleep away any of her new concerns, when the very man destroying her peace stepped around the corner.

"Lady Evaline." He nodded his head. "Am I correct in assuming this is your quarters?"

"Yes, it is."

"It's early. Are you retiring?"

"I think I must."

"Must?" He approached. "Why must you?"

She studied him. He seemed perfectly romantically uninterested. Perhaps Lady Constance was seeing things that just weren't there. "Might I ask you a question?"

"Certainly. But perhaps we might walk to another corridor." He indicated her bedroom door.

"Oh. Of course." She placed a hand on his arm, and he led them to the other end. They stood in front of a window. A bright moon rose up over the lawn out behind the house. Eva's nerves still were just as tight, but she made an attempt at light conversation. "It really is such a beautiful estate."

"Thank you for inviting me here. I didn't tell you that it came at a perfect time for me."

"Why?"

"Edward keeps talking about me getting married, my saving money, me making a name for myself."

She stiffened.

"But I'm not marrying. And what do I know about making a name for myself?"

Her breath trickled out in a great relief. "So, you are still not interested in marrying?"

"Correct." His gaze flit to hers and then lingered a moment. "Why do you ask?"

"Oh, I don't really ask, just... I avoid men who have any inclination to marry..." She watched his face.

"You... avoid men..." His gaze lingered on her face, and she watched while he tried to figure her out. "Are you wondering if I..." He pointed to her and then back to him, his eyebrows raising. "Lady Evaline. We hardly know one another." He shook his head.

She nodded slowly. "Well, thank you for assuring me of your intentions."

"You're welcome." A great awkward air descended between them, and Eva could tell Mr. Easton wanted only to be parted from her. She must make some excuse for him to leave her.

"I'm feeling tired."

"Yes, of course." He led her back down the hall toward her room. They heard voices coming up the stairs.

"Perhaps I shall wait here while you make your way to your bedroom door?" Mr. Easton indicated the sound.

"Yes, thank you. I'll see you tomorrow?"

"Certainly. I heard we might ride horses or take a tour of the estate."

She nodded, then turned from him and hurried to her room, more confused than ever. Was she relieved? He obviously did not think of her in the way Lady Constance suggested.

Yes. She was relieved. Wasn't she? Of course. She stepped into her room, closed the door, and told Remy she wished to dress for bed.

Chapter Eight

O scar lifted his chin while his valet untied his cravat. "She's a complete puzzle, Reed. The woman makes no sense to me at all. And she had me singing a duet. A *duet*. Can you envision such a thing?"

"I cannot, sir." Reed collected the fabric from Oscar's cravat. "Might I ask, are you a proficient?"

Oscar huffed. "Do *you* think I might be a proficient?"

"It is not my place to say." Reed never broke character, not ever. Even now, his lip didn't twitch though Oscar suspected he found the idea of his employer singing a duet highly amusing.

Oscar laughed. "You can safely assume I am not."

Reed folded his jacket over his arm and helped him out of his shirt. "I have a pitcher of water. Would you like me to draw a bath as well?"

"No. Tomorrow for that. We will ride horses."

"Very good, sir."

Reed left him, walking through the closet into his own room, a tiny offshoot of the closet. They were both pleased with this arrangement as in some houses, the servants were relegated to servants' quarters which may or may not have been fitting for large groups.

Oscar found himself quite impressed in most respects with this house party.

He awoke the next morning early, deciding to ride with the gentlemen at the party. Reed told him that he'd learned from the other valets that a group of them were going out early with the hope to really ride, go a farther distance and perhaps see if there would be good reason to try a hunt during the course of the party.

Once he was dressed in his riding gear, he hurried to the breakfast room where a few men were filling plates. As he approached, Mr. Shaw took notice. "Ah, Mr. Easton, is it?"

The others turned to size him up.

"Yes, I heard talk of a good ride this morning and wondered if there was room for one more?"

"Certainly." The man nearest Oscar turned with a full plate to sit at the table. When Oscar joined him, he held out a hand. "Lucas Stanhope."

"Ah, great to meet you. Oscar Easton."

"Edward's brother?"

"The one and the same." Oscar tried not to feel irritated.

"There are three of you Easton's, correct?"

"Yes. With our sister."

Mr. Stanhope nodded his head. "Not one of you married yet, I hear?"

"Just our sister. To Lord Hamilton."

"Oh yes, the best of men. I ran into him last month in London." Lord Stanhope sipped something warm from his cup, likely coffee.

"I think they were there to discuss something with a committee in Parliament. They're at our family seat now to spend Christmas."

Mr. Stanhope eyed him. "And you all the way up here instead?"

"I needed some space."

"Well, you'll find it here. Nothing but rocky green beauty in any direction."

Another joined them, a tall broad-shouldered man. "Lord Knightsbridge." He nodded and took his first bite.

After introductions and breakfast, they soon found themselves out on horses behind the back paddock. Five men in all. Lord Stanhope, Lord Knightsbridge and Oscar were joined by two others, each an excellent seat on a horse. They rode out together, tearing across an open field. And Oscar reveled in the freedom. Every day should feel just like this one. Why could he never feel so at ease any longer when at home with his brother?

Their group gathered at the top of a ridge, overlooking all of the estate. "From here you can see the whole of it, gentlemen." Lord Knightsbridge acted as their guide since he'd been to Ivy Manor the most.

They talked about specific tenants and property yield until Oscar began to feel as though they were at auction. When at last they moved on to other topics, he brought his attention back to the front.

"What do you know of our fellow guests at the party?" Lord Knightbridge's horse started to tap his feet.

Oscar, too, was anxious for a ride.

"The ladies are exceptional in title, rank, breeding." Lord Knightsbridge acted as though he were listing off qualities of a good brood mare. Oscar felt a touch uncomfortable for the fairer sex.

"If you can stomach past Lady Snow."

"Who?" Oscar leaned forward.

They shared a look. "He doesn't even know."

"We thought you'd recognize her nickname the moment we mentioned it."

"I don't understand." Oscar adjusted his seat.

"As her particular friend…" He laughed and the others did too.

"Lady Evaline? Lady Snow?" He frowned.

"Now, don't get all itchy inside." Lord Knightsbridge clucked. "If you haven't seen it yet, you will."

"Seen what?"

"Her ice, her cold shoulder."

Lord Stanhope shook his head and leaned forward on his saddle. "Yes, I'll spell it out. You're getting to know her. You're both happy. She seems to enjoy your attentions. You try to take it to the next step and then… ice."

The others hissed.

Oscar looked from one to the other. "Meaning?"

"She shuts you down." Lord Stanhope held up one finger and ran it across his throat.

"Everyone?"

"Two of us, and practically everyone we know." Knightsbridge leaned forward. "She was engaged once. Took it all the way to the altar and then cancelled at the last minute, banns had been read, everything planned. Rumor has it she still has the dress. But there aren't very many more men she can push away." He shrugged. "You must not be to the part where you try to take things to the next place."

"Nor will we be." Oscar shook his head. "We are friends, and just barely that."

They eyed him with enough suspicion that he felt like

he needed to explain. "I just don't see her that way. And if what you say is true, there has to be a reason. From what I can tell, she's not like that."

They snorted. "From what we could tell, she wasn't either." Lord Stanhope turned his horse. "Ask Lord Thomason. He can give you an earful of how she totally blindsided him and ended their engagement."

"She's not much to look at but she has a huge dowry. If any man can get past her face and ever win her heart, he'll be drowning in money, as well as his children and their children after."

Anger burned at the back of his throat, but he said nothing. Not much to look at? He thought her quite handsome. Oscar considered everything they said. But he didn't know what to make of it. They rode the rest of the morning. He took his horse as fast as she would go. By the time he returned to the house, his curiosity about Lady Evaline still tickled his thoughts, but he felt much better than he had since he arrived.

The women were gathered outside in small groups with parasols when he and the others returned. Lady Evaline nodded at him which he barely returned and hurried into the house. What to make of this woman? Do the others speak the truth? Is this a wild and unfair rumor spread by a few slighted lords? He didn't want to be involved in the matter.

Reed directed the filling of his bath which he was most grateful for. Once the sweat and horse were washed thoroughly from his person, he sat to write a letter home. He felt a ping of loneliness for the Easton's during the holidays. Who to write? Tabitha. At the end, as an afterthought, he penned the question most on his mind. "Who is Lady Evaline? What do we know of her?"

The evening and then morning of the next day passed before he talked to her again. But he certainly saw her. Every time he looked around, he saw her, or at least it seemed so. She painted with the other women. She laughed with women at the breakfast table. She walked with them in the gardens. And talked in the library with women. Not a single man ever came near her. Or if they did, they left soon after. He couldn't figure her out.

But why did he need to? He laughed at himself. And then went to find her because he really did wish to understand this woman. She wasn't in the front parlor where ladies were doing needlepoint. Lord Stanhope sat in there and was a great entertainer if judged by the smiling, laughing women around him. She wasn't in the library or the card room or at the piano. He asked a maid. "Have you seen Lady Evaline?"

"Yes, sir. I think she went outside to the gardens."

She was immediately visible among the roses. She wore green again today. The kind of bright green that stood out in almost any location. But her hair was simple. Curls lined her face and one long braid rested on her shoulder. For a moment he forgot where he was and watched a fairylike woman wander among the flowers.

But she saw him and smiled. "There you are."

He picked up his pace. "How are you?"

"I'm doing well. This is a nice party I think, so far." Her eyes held questions. "What do you think?"

"It's been interesting." He stood at her side. "Could we walk?"

"Certainly. I've not seen the farthest east side of these gardens."

They walked for a moment, standing apart. She seemed to be lost in her thoughts. In his mind, he started and stopped a seemingly hundred different topics. Their conversation from earlier replayed in his mind. She avoids men who are interested in marriage. From all appearances, she avoids men in general. But that was simply contrary to a woman's happiness, wasn't it? Surely, she wished to marry... someday. His breath huffed out without his meaning it to. "And why don't you wish to marry?"

She nearly stumbled.

He stepped closer and offered his arm. It was an automatic response, but she hesitated, searching his face before placing the barest pressure on his sleeve.

"I don't wish to marry, at this time, simply because I don't." She looked away and kept walking for a moment as if that answer would ever be a sufficient one.

"It isn't my business of course, but if you are to announce me as your particular friend, I might need to have a socially acceptable reason ready to respond." There. That was the gist of things.

"Have people been asking?"

He paused. They approached a fountain. "Might I speak frankly?"

"Certainly."

"The men talk. They wonder at your mannerisms with them."

"How so?"

"I believe the word, Lady Snow, was used."

Her face closed off for a moment. "Let me guess, were any the particular friends of Lord Thomason?"

"Some. I understand you broke off that engagement, but the others spoke from experience. They say you shut men out of your life if they become too close to you?"

She turned to him. They stood closer than he realized. But he didn't step away. She didn't answer for a moment, so he continued. "I thought I would mention… suggest… that you warm up to them a little bit."

"Warm up?" She tilted her head.

"Yes, you know, smile and encourage conversation. They aren't going to ask to take you down the aisle within moments of you being cordial."

The area around her jaw clenched and moved. Was she grinding her teeth?

"And so, you think I should encourage them? These men?"

"Well, encourage… is perhaps not the best word, but be cordial. Like I do with the women." He placed a hand over hers in an attempt to soften his no doubt intrusive comments.

"I don't allow relationships to grow when I know there will be no purpose to them." Her nose rise higher in the air.

He nodded. "I can understand. And that includes friendships?"

"It wouldn't. If men could simply be friends. Every single one starts out a lovely friendship and soon after begins declaring their love." She lifted her eyelashes. "And that is the reason for my rather awkward question to you the other evening. Someone asked me the nature of our relationship. She thought…" Lady Evaline's face turned the deepest red and Oscar was immediately glued to her every word. "She thought you besotted."

Oscar closed his eyes and counted slowly in his mind. Of all the ridiculously foolhardy womanly things to assume. "I'm most certainly not besotted." He stopped just short of calling such an idea ridiculous. No need to insult the woman. "You are, of course, a lovely woman. Your face and your hair, attractive. I could never call you anything but desirable, but no. I am not besotted."

"Excellent. That is welcome news indeed." She tilted her head. "But you and I have discussed this already. Why is it coming up anew?"

"When men ask me about your sudden tendency to be cold to them, should I simply explain that you are rather particular in choosing your friendships?"

"That is perfect. And when women question your degree of infatuation?"

"You can tell them the truth. That we hardly know each other. That you asked for my attendance as a favor and that we have a growing friendship, that is all."

She nodded; a flash of disappointment muddied her otherwise obvious relief.

"But why? As your friend and for no other reason, I would like to know why you behave so? Why do you wish to discourage men?"

She turned away and began walking. "I have my reasons. And they are personal."

He nodded. He could respect such a thing as privacy. "Is there a man at this party you would like me to speak to on your behalf? To give a little encouragement?"

"Heavens no!" Her expression of horror, the depth of panic that filled her face, shocked him. But he said nothing more. "Understood."

"I will take my leave now. But I heard we are assembling food and supplies for local families and they asked us to pair up. Would you like to be my partner for the activity?"

"Yes, I would. And thank you."

He nodded and then turned on his heels to leave her be. For whatever reason, he couldn't make his legs move quickly enough. His hands shook. What on earth did he have to be afraid of in Lady Evaline? He turned back.

She was looking up into the sky. Her lovely slender neck, creamy and visible in the warm sun. Her arms hung at her side. Her hair glistened. She was an appealing picture. What man would ever think her anything but beautiful? He pushed on, away from the sight. Was he walking away because of his new and alarming attraction to the woman? He shook his head. Who had thought him besotted? Did he look besotted?

As he analyzed his behavior over the last few days, he found no evidence of outward interest beyond friendship, but plenty of thoughts directed her way. He would not. He refused to accept that he was in any way interested in something with Lady Evaline. Thoughts directed toward her were natural. She was an astounding woman.

And yet, he forced every movement of his feet away from her, forced because a strange impulse to run back to her side now battled the effort.

Chapter Nine

Cold. She shook her head. She should be glad they talked about her as cold. They might keep their distance if the talk persisted. But… did they have to call her *Lady Snow*? She squirmed, twisting her hands together at her front. And Mr. Easton had encouraged her to warm up? To be friendly? He agreed with their cold assessment then. He must or else why suggest she change her behavior? She tore a leaf off the nearest tree. He had no idea what he was talking about. She paced the gardens. Perhaps an even more outlandish presentation? More distraction? She paused. She paced again. Thoughts raced through her mind and she found it difficult to keep up with her own emotion.

She was perfectly polite. If she "warmed up" to these men they would respond in kind, and every one of them would assume she had a new interest in a relationship. Is that what Mr. Easton wanted? And why must they discuss her at all? Could she not be left alone? She tried to pretend otherwise, but people thinking about her, talking about her, forming opinions about why she did things made her supremely uncomfortable. And, to be honest, she'd just rather everyone held her in high esteem. This new word, snow, well, it didn't sit well. Not at all. Her irritation grew. What did they expect her to do? All this time, she'd thought her new style had distracted them.

Mr. Easton thought her ridiculous. Would he enjoy the alternative? Let him see what a little warming up could do. Perhaps he wouldn't care at all that the men at the house party might start hovering about. But at least he would notice, and she could make her point.

She'd rather be thinking of the service activity than giving attention to a bunch of money seeking men. She would simply participate in such a worthy cause without concerning herself with these new troubling concerns. She was so looking forward to aiding local needy families. And what better partner than Mr. Easton. She smiled in spite of her frustration. After the service activity, she might follow his advice and warm up to some of them. Though she dreaded even the thought.

But then, she'd show him what happened when she smiled a little more. These men were all mercenary, every one of them. One smile, especially after being indifferent for so long, could very well change whatever life plans they had previously. She couldn't blame them, she supposed. It would be hard to turn away a dowry of her size, even if they couldn't abide her face. A sudden flood of emotion surprised her, though it shouldn't. The lump in her throat grew and she didn't even try to wipe away the moisture at her eyes. A small bench on the far side welcomed her tired body. As soon as she sat, her head fell into her hands and she slumped her shoulders. She was tired. Tired of making excuses and tired of blaming herself, tired of others putting blame on her. And tired of running. Mr. Easton would soon see. And maybe he would understand.

If only she could go back to her first Season. Her hopeful heart and starry eyes had entered every ballroom looking for the love of her life. If only she could have found it and skipped over the wretched years of heartache after.

Heartache had shown himself in the form of cravat-tying, hessian-wearing handsomeness, and she'd fallen for him after a paltry amount of attention thrown her way. Looking back, it was far simpler to understand. Curse her naiveté. She'd fallen in love faster than she thought possible. And for a brief two months, she'd been far happier than she thought a person could be. Her fiancé was perfect. He doted on her in every way. It was easy to understand his dedication when she found out why.

Eva stood. Enough was enough. She would put this nonsense behind her, once and for all. She would move forward with a happy life. As she'd told plenty of people before, a wealthy woman could afford to be alone and happy.

But her heart ached at the thought. And as much as she tried to talk herself into the new mantra, *happiness is being alone,* the lie tormented her peace. She couldn't face what she most desperately yearned for with every breath. She *must not* believe in love. She had learned that love wasn't possible for her. She'd tried and seen the ugly claws of heartbreak. No love was worth the risk of any of those claws leaving their mark again.

She'd met all the men here at the house party at one time or another. She was in no danger of falling in love with any of them, and now that she knew that they talked of her, called her names, the temptation to show them for who they are was too great. Let their true sides be seen. At least to Mr. Easton. She had a feeling he would see clearly what everyone was about when they started doting and sitting beside her and paying her attention of all kinds. Why was she willing to go to such lengths to prove something to Mr. Easton?

Her heart pounded in her chest. But she huffed and walked faster. Because she hated that he thought ill of her. She was tired of her loneliness. If only one person understood her plight, then let it be Mr. Easton.

The next day everyone who wished to participate gathered in what looked like the ballroom. Servants ran in and out of the room, still carrying in supplies. Her eyes scanned the room. Mr. Easton. Mr. Easton. Mr. Easton. Ah, there he was. She took steps in his direction but not before she was nearly trampled over by three men, Mr. Talmus leading the bunch.

His eyes widened as if expecting a talking down to, which she might ordinarily have administered—or at least a snub. Such a reaction would have been merited. They did nearly knock her to the ground.

"I beg your pardon." He bowed low.

"Not at all, of course." She smiled her most charming smile.

Mr. Talmus looked as though he struggled to swallow for a moment or two, his throat bobbing away with great difficulty. Then he straightened and nodded to her again.

"I think it rather gallant that the three of you are so intent upon helping the tenants that you are hurrying so." She smiled again and then made her way over to Mr. Easton who, as luck would have it, was watching with great amusement on his face.

She didn't dare turn around. And she couldn't fathom

what he found so entertaining, but she hoped to sit beside him and begin their work.

"Oh stop. You can close your mouth now." She sat and pulled the basket toward her.

"I don't know what you did, but you've got three men struck like stone in the middle of the room staring."

"Oh, they're not still staring, are they?"

"Yes, they are. And they don't even notice that I'm staring back or obviously talking about them." He waved his hand. "Nope. Didn't notice that either."

"Let's just begin, shall we?"

"What did you say to them?" He finally turned away from the men and toward her.

"Nothing. Well, just that I appreciate that they were so intent on helping the poor they hurried into the room and nearly knocked me over. I said it was rather gallant."

He pressed his lips together. "You were much too nice. They deserved the set down I know was on the edge of your tongue."

"But someone told me to be more... warm."

He studied her and looked toward the men again and then said nothing.

"What? Changing your mind?"

"Warmth and politeness. Both are good things."

She reached for the bread. "Is there a list? What goes in each basket?"

He fumbled for a moment and then produced a list. "Bread."

"Yes, I've added that."

"Right. Now nuts and dried fruit."

They rummaged through the supplies and found bundles of nuts and the dried fruit. Soon they were adding Christmas pudding and cooks' biscuits.

Mr. Easton held onto the last bundle of biscuits, studying it. "What do you suppose…"

"What do you mean?"

"What sort of biscuits?"

"Sort…."

He began to unwrap the package.

"You will not." She reached for it, but he held it slightly out of reach.

"That." She straightened and ran her hands down her skirt. "That isn't for you."

"They won't miss it." His eyes twinkled. He was enjoying tormenting her. She looked away for a second, drawn to his enjoyment more powerfully than she thought healthy. Then totally surprised him as she lunged across him and snatched the biscuits. But she lost her balance, laughing, and she fell into him.

He put his hands on her waist, right at her hips and tipped her back up right. "Easy now. Are you hungry? What is this? Perhaps we can share these lovely biscuits."

She tried to ignore the interested gazes of the others around them. "We cannot. Those are for the tenants. I'm certain if you want a biscuit you can ask any one of these servants and they will offer you jam as well."

"Oh, very well. Perhaps I shall do so before we make our deliveries. I shouldn't like to faint from hunger on the way."

She laughed again. Something about Mr. Easton, teasing, joking, was tying her stomach up in pleasant knots. And her waist, her hips, the whole area he'd touched tingled. She was drawn to him, wanting his hands back around her. She tried not to analyze it overmuch. They had a work to do, and they best be about doing it.

"Let's fill our other baskets, and then we'll be off."

They filled two more and while Mr. Easton went in search of the direction and a cart to use, she tried to compose herself. She steadied her breathing. She was not enjoying Mr. Easton's company. She snorted. Of course she was. But she could enjoy a man's company and not turn that into some lovesick longing she'd vowed to never feel again.

Eyes watched her. She was used to the sensation, but she turned anyway. Mr. Talmus. He and his table were all watching, assessing, more like. And she didn't love the feeling of their gazes crawling around on her skin. But she didn't turn away with a huff. Instead, she smiled a bland, pleasant sort of reaction and then turned away.

Before she could think about walking to find Mr. Easton, she felt Mr. Talmus and the others approach.

She turned, slowly, trying to regain her smile. "Oh, hello. We've finished early. Mr. Easton's gone to find us a cart."

"We saw you with Mr. Easton. Something's different about you, Lady Evaline." Mr. Talmus studied her face and then he winked. "I might be interested in getting to know this new side of her ladyship."

"Oh? Hmm. Well, I'm the same as ever."

He stepped closer. "Do you think she's the same as ever, gentlemen?"

Her skin tingled in a whole new undesirable way, and she wished to run or snub them or insult them—anything to get them farther away. But she was at a loss as to what to say in response. Before she had to make those choices, Mr. Easton returned. "Are we ready?" He stepped right in between her and Mr. Talmus. She almost laughed but instead put her hand on Mr. Easton's arm and hurried them both from the room. "Thank you," she whispered.

"What are they after?" Oscar asked.

"Don't tell me you don't know what they're after."

"Fine, but why are they after it with such a singular intent?" He looked over his shoulder.

"Because I smiled at him when I walked into the room."

"Really?" He looked like he might not believe her.

"Yes, that's what I'm trying to show you."

"Hmm. I'm not certain this is merely a reaction to your smile. But whatever the reason, they stood too close, with too proprietary an air. And I didn't like it."

"Nor I." She shivered and stood closer to Mr. Easton. "But let's forget about them and enjoy our outing, shall we?"

"Yes, most definitely." He brought them to a cart pulled by a donkey. Another maid had joined them. "I've brought us help and a conveyance. We are ready to make our deliveries." He made a mocking bow and then helped her up inside.

She tried to brush aside how nice it felt to have a trustworthy man at her side, to feel safe and cared for, to have enjoyable conversation and to feel that even if she smiled, Mr. Easton wasn't going to fall in love and propose tomorrow and she couldn't get used to the idea of him in her life.

Chapter Ten

Mr. Easton tried to look at Lady Evaline just how he had always looked at her. But he couldn't forget the feel of her waist in his hands. She was nice to hold. Her waist was small, soft, her hips wider than he expected. The tingling from their interaction lingered still. And then the pleased expression in her eyes. She'd felt something too. He reached for the reins. He would conquer this or else turn into a lovesick pup following after Lady Evaline like the others.

And Mr. Easton wasn't lovesick over anyone, had no desire to marry, and was at this very point in time actively seeking for ways to earn a living. He had no time and was completely unprepared to pursue a marriage.

"What are you thinking?"

"Hmm?" He startled at the very subject of his thoughts interrupted. "Nothing really, about delivering baskets I suppose?"

"You frown while delivering baskets to tenants? No. Something troubles you."

He studied her and decided to share a bit of himself. Perhaps she might have a good idea or two. "I think I need to converse more with Mr. Shaw."

"I am all astonishment. Why?"

"Because." He guided their donkey down a narrow lane. "I should like to earn a proper inheritance for my children. I'd like an estate of my own. To make a name for myself in any other way than marrying into money." He dipped his head. "Apologies if that offends."

"Offends? On the contrary. I find it so highly refreshing that I am further astonished. You, Mr. Easton, are a man of many surprises."

"Don't be too impressed or place too much honor on my head. My brother is the eldest. And this action stems merely from the frustration of having to go to him for an increase in my allowance."

"And the part about not marrying your wealth?"

"Well, now that part just seems fair. I would like to bring something to my future estate as well." He cleared his throat. Her eyes were too wide and too smiling and altogether too... something. "Not that I'm considering any sort of path to marriage at the moment."

"Of course not, which is why we are so well suited."

"Pardon me?" He searched her face. "Did you just say, we're well suited?"

"Yes, for this party. I chose the very best person to come assist me."

"Well, you wrote at the perfect moment," Oscar confided.

"How so?"

"I'd just come from a particularly aggravating conversation with my brother. My valet was packing for us to leave. I hadn't decided where to spend my time, and your letter arrived that very day in my hands."

"Then we shall thank providence for directing us." Her soft sigh and the tiniest pucker of her lips filled him with a desire to move her closer to him on the bench of this rickety old cart, so that he could put his arm around her.

"And what brings on your frown?"

"Oh, nothing I suppose. Right now, everything is perfectly enjoyable. We are doing something I most love, with the only man I enjoy being with, at Christmastime in the home of my dear great-uncle whose company I enjoy. I should be perfectly satisfied."

The only man she enjoyed being with. He sat taller. He felt an undeniable pride in that unique place in her life. "Then I am meeting your hopes as a friend at the party?"

"Yes, greatly exceeding them, certainly. Thank you. And I shall try to be more pleasant to the others so that you aren't left explaining away awkward conversations."

Remembering the way the Lords approached her, Oscar started to shake his head. But they had arrived at the first tenants, and she was already waving and calling out to the house.

A small family gathered at the door. Lady Evaline jumped from the cart and hurried to them. "Hello. How is everyone today?" She got down at eye level with the children. "We've brought baskets, but now I wish I had toys."

"Oh no, my lady. We are so grateful for the baskets." A woman stood next to her husband. "The crops didn't come in like they should, and we're needing all the assistance through these cold winter months."

"I'm just pleased that Mr. Shaw has made it possible to help in the delivery. It is through his kindness that this is possible."

Listening to the family and Lady Evaline converse kindled the beginnings of a new fire inside Oscar. He would love to be able to do so much, to offer assistance, in the way that Mr. Shaw was able.

They finished out the afternoon delivering baskets, and with every home and every grateful response from needy families, Oscar felt a greater desire to have the resources to do such a thing himself. So much so, that when he kissed Lady Evaline's hand in farewell, his mind was already thinking about where he might find Mr. Shaw.

As he walked away, her voice carried forward. "You wish an audience with my uncle?"

He turned his head back to her. "Yes, as a matter of fact, I am much distracted by just such a thing." How could she know?

"Let's go find him directly."

"Excellent."

She placed her hands on his arm in the friendliest gesture, but after an afternoon full of her lovely face, her caring gestures, her playing with children and spoon feeding the poor, he was unable to feel unaffected by her touch. It would pass, he hoped, but for now, his task was to pretend he didn't notice the exceptionally beautiful woman at his side or her cool fingers resting on his arm.

"Most people don't know. But he finds pleasure in a small sitting room outside the library."

"Ah, very good." He allowed her to lead him along, grateful again for yet another opportunity in regards to Lady Evaline.

They stood at the entrance to the smaller sitting room. "I see why he enjoys this room so much."

"Yes, it is lovely. A library, but with more light." She smiled and tugged on his arm to enter.

He hesitated. "I feel a bit like we are intruding."

"Nonsense. He'll be along."

They moved into a quaint room with comfortable chairs, a fire blazing in the grate and garland all about the place.

"I hear the servants will be decorating this afternoon. We're welcome to join them."

Oscar chuckled. "I am the one at home that puts garland up around the front entrance."

"Are you? I'm in charge of the fireplaces."

They sat together on a small settee. He was grateful she didn't choose a different chair further from him. The closeness felt comforting and supremely unsettling in a pleasant sort of way. He couldn't make her out, but he didn't want her to move. When her hand brushed his arm, or their shoulders touched, he was pleasantly unsettled again and again.

"Tell me more about yourself." He surprised even himself with the question, but suddenly finding out everything he could in regards to this woman at his side had become the most important part of his visit.

"Well, I'm an only child."

"Ah, I wouldn't know what that's like with my brother and sister always near as children."

Her wistful sigh made him just a little bit more grateful for his busy household.

"What is your family's estate like?"

"It's lovely. Not like this place. There are no rocks and crags and hills about, but we have large areas of grass and trees. It is quite flat until you reach the cliffs. And then the sea stretches out to the horizon."

"Brighton?"

"No. We're in the Northeast. Our property abuts a rocky cliff."

"You sound like you miss the water."

"Oh, I do. I would spend every second there if I could."

"And why aren't you there for Christmas?"

Her face looked pained for a moment and then it cleared. "My father thought it important I attend this party. He wishes to keep up relations." She turned soft, wide eyes to him. "I fear he is as mercenary as the rest." Her soft whisper sunk deep inside. He longed for her to say something else in that husky, soft manner.

"But you aren't."

She shook her head. "Not at all. We have enough." Her tone said too much. But he didn't bring up their other uncomfortable conversation, didn't want to talk about all the money in her dowry.

"And I came because Uncle Shaw is a dear."

"I saw a young lad in the window. Is he about?" Oscar wasn't sure why he was reminded of the lad in this moment. But he'd been curious.

"Oh, he's the most darling boy. I visit him in the mornings to help with his schooling."

"You do?" Oscar couldn't have been more surprised. "Are you a great admirer of children?"

"is that so difficult to believe?" She shook her head. "I adore them." The sigh that followed seemed to stem from deep inside, from places of great pain. He wasn't sure he wished to ask, but he did want to alleviate something of her hurt. Words failed him. She had no siblings, no hopes to be an aunt. She was without recourse unless she wished to marry, which, he certainly had no wish to bring up again.

"He's a blessed lad then."

Her eyes met his and the unspoken understanding that passed between them, gratitude on her end and compassion on his, felt powerful. It changed him somehow and he determined to be her friend, to defend her, to assist here when he could.

"Would you look at this cozy scene." Mr. Talmus stood in the doorway, leaning against the frame. "Looking for our host? Hope to charm him with your wiles?"

"My…" Lady Evaline's small confused pout raked against Oscar's well-being.

"What do you want, Talmus?"

"Want? I'd like to join you."

Oscar almost groaned.

But Lady Evaline surprised him by standing. "We were just leaving." She swayed a moment as if about to fall. And Oscar leapt up to steady her. "Are you all right?"

"I don't know. I've never had an almost swoon."

Mr. Talmus snorted. "I have that effect."

"Yes, thank you, Talmus." Oscar led her from the room, brushing past the man who looked too closely at the woman he cradled in his arms. "Where can I take you?" he murmured close to her ear.

"To the kitchen." she whispered, this time her voice laced with humor.

He looked down into her face, close to his own. "Are you not even unwell?"

"Hush. Hurry."

He shook his head. "To think I fell for your act."

"Oh, come now. Was that not fun? To rescue a woman about to swoon?"

To himself only, he admitted he quite enjoyed himself; but to her, he shook his head. "You are a troublesome creature."

Her laugh started small as a beautiful tinkling sound,

and then filled the hall as they made their way into the kitchen.

"Do you still wish to be here?" They entered a busy and loud place. Cook was preparing something that smelled amazing. His stomach complained of want.

She approached the nearest servant. "Might we trouble you for a biscuit or two?"

"Yes, my lady." The girl bobbed a curtsey and prepared a tin, jam, and biscuits on a tray, more than the two of them could possibly eat. "Will there be anything else, my lady?"

"No, thank you." Lady Evaline's triumphant smile made him laugh and almost won his forgiveness for her deceit, well-timed though it was.

They hurried from the kitchen and encountered Lady Fenning and Lady Constance. Though Oscar preferred time alone with Lady Evaline, he smiled openly. "We have become the beneficiaries of quite a large tray of biscuits. Would you care to join us?"

Soon all three were seated at a table in the library.

Lady Evaline shifted in her seat as she talked with one lady or the other. Her energy seemed to know no bounds. Her laughter was warm and inviting. Her smiles large. The more he studied her the more he appreciated that she was not alone by natural inclinations. She did not wish to be apart from the others. In fact, she craved attention and interaction. The thought pleased him to no end. Perhaps it was the company that brought out her more relaxed and engaging nature. These two women were of high quality both in their situations and also in their natures. At least that was his impression. Watching them all converse confirmed to him his initial impressions. When Lady Evaline said something particularly funny, they all laughed openly. She turned to him with such a look of joy, his responding smile was immediate. His body thundered in response to the beauty before him. He'd always thought her nice looking, a bit eccentric and intriguing, but how had he not noticed her breath-stealing beauty? Why was every man at the party not clamoring for her attention? Was he besotted? No, certainly not. He would never go so far as to think such a thing, but no matter what anyone else thought, she was definitely appealing, something he couldn't admit to her or anyone else at this point.

Chapter Eleven

For the next two days, Eva busied herself wherever Mr. Easton wasn't. His looks, his touch, still imprinted on her memory. Oh, she was in danger indeed. She couldn't, wouldn't, fall for another man. Particularly one who was not at all interested in marriage. Would she break her heart again—this time pining for someone who had no interest, not even in her dowry?

But had he no interest? His expression said otherwise, possibly. She had no way of knowing. She had no trust in her ability to read the male mind. She'd been so certain years ago that Lord Thomason was in love. How could she know? Mr. Easton seemed attentive. He smiled. He sat close, so close. She shivered in remembrance of her yearning for his touch.

Her head shook. No. She could not be entertaining these thoughts. She would never accept his attentions were he to offer them. She trembled—out of fear or anticipation she no longer knew. She simply could not understand her own or his feelings. Preserve her heart and move on as a spinster had been her plan, and she was going to stick with it forever. She grit her teeth. No matter what.

Unable to sit still, she made her way to the stables. The air had taken an icy turn. Winter had come upon them at last. And the air… it smelled of snow. Would they have a lovely white dressing on everything around them before the end of the party? Servants saddled a mare for her, a sandy colored beauty named Magic. Eva wanted to rest her cheek on her soft nose. But the horse stomped with an energy that Eva also felt. So much so that the second she was up in the saddle, she took off out of the stable area, through the smaller corral and onto the open land. The shouts behind her fell on deaf ears. Was she wise to go out all by herself? She was probably fine. The icy wind numbed her cheeks. The tips of her ears hurt. Wind whipped through her hair. Soon all pins were lost, and her hair trailed out behind. Her mare shared her energy and tore ever faster up a hill behind the house and to the very top ridge. She pulled the reins. "Whoa, Miss. Whoa. We're going to take a look here for a minute."

Magic seemed to want to fight her halt in the wild freedom; her flank quivered and her feet stamped, but she waited.

Eva looked out over the land all around. Mr. Shaw had a beautiful estate. She was happy for him. And sad at the same time. He missed his previous wife dearly. And who loved him most now of all these grasping relatives? Who cared for the man with no interest in his wealth? She understood him at a deep level and vowed not to ask her uncle for a single thing. They were alike in this. She understood his potential loneliness. Who cared for her with no interest in her wealth?

Her face pinched but she refused to give in to the great

loneliness that threatened or the tears that might freeze on her face. She shivered. "Come on, girl."

The horse leapt at her command, and they raced over the ridge and across the lands on the other side. Everything around them was beautiful in a rocky, craggy sort of way. The horse seemed to know how to navigate the uneven ground, so Eva allowed her the freedom to run as she pleased.

The wild exhilaration distracted her but did nothing to solve her confusion. She raced longer, pushed Magic harder. Somehow she would win. She would resist feelings for Mr. Easton and she would be happy in her lonely state. She would find satisfaction in other ways.

And she could, too. She had. Her life was lovely. Until she'd seen Mr. Easton care for her, until she'd seen him with the tenants, until she'd felt his hands at her hips. Just the memory of it caused a rush of warmth. She'd never felt anything similar with Lord Thomason. Had she even loved that man? Certainly. Perhaps, but nothing like she felt for Mr. Easton had ever happened with him. Did she love Mr. Easton or was she merely entrapped by a strange sort of lonely attraction?

Her ride, meant to clear her mind and appreciate the quiet suddenly felt lackluster and… she admitted, lonely. But she was miles from the house

A shout on the wind behind her made her turn. A lone figure on a black horse tore across the wide-open space. She squinted her eyes. For a moment, her nerves rose. Who was coming? Who rode so quickly? But then she recognized Mr. Easton's hair and the breadth of his shoulders. "What the devil." She smiled at her language no governess would allow. She slowed her horse. And she waited.

He was a brilliant horseman. His horse shone in the sun, the brilliant black a pleasing contrast to the tan of his riding habit. His body seemed to glide with the movement, completely comfortable even at such a high speed.

But he came too soon. She had no idea yet how to handle her new feelings. She studied his approaching figure. He waved, his smile almost visible at this distance. A new sensation clenched in her stomach, a happy hopeful expectation, and she could only smile. A great laugh grew from that clenching in her stomach, bubbled out of her and filled the air. This delicious joy was something to welcome, surely?

By the time he arrived at her side, almost as out of breath as his horse, he laughed. "What is this smile? You look as though Christmas has already arrived."

She calmed her dancing horse. "I'm just happy to see you."

"This is for me?" He appraised her, his eyes lighting in fascinating ways. "I'm honored." He dipped his head.

"Oh, don't be. I rode out here for over an hour and suddenly realized a bit of company would be nice."

"So, any company would do? Should I fetch Mr. Talmus?"

"Not at all." She looked down and then made a decision… of sorts. "Not any company. It was yours that was most pleasing in this moment."

He seemed to rise in his saddle. His shoulders broadened, and he puffed. "As it should be." Then he grinned. "You were flying. It took me the better part of thirty minutes to catch you." He patted his horse. "Good thing the horses seem born to ride."

"Yes, Magic here was anxious to get out on the land."

"Shall we walk a moment though? I think he needs to keep moving so he doesn't seize up."

"Oh yes, certainly."

They rode, side by side. And though she tried not to, her smile kept reappearing.

"Please tell me the source of this smile. It cannot simply be that I now ride beside you."

"How did you find me? Or even know where I was?"

"I was needing a ride myself. I think I arrived at the stables shortly after you and a very determined and caring stablemaster informed me of your grave indiscretion."

"Which was?"

"To ride out without a footman. He was preparing one, but I told him that I would take care of it. None of us could see you, you were so quickly up and over the ridge."

She laughed. "I shall have to suggest the stablemaster receive a little extra for his efforts. That was a kind thing to do."

"Yes, and he might still be coming. I don't know if he completely trusted my ability to keep you safe."

"Perhaps he wondered if you were something to be protected from."

He laughed. "I do think you might have something there."

"And are you?"

"Am I what?"

"Something I need to be wary of? Is my reputation at risk?" She raised one eyebrow, laughing again with her eyes. Was she flirting? Indeed, she was. The whole concept felt thrilling.

And to her delight, he rode a little closer, leaned across so that she could almost feel the heat off of him. His curls were damp from the ride and all over his head in the wind. "That depends."

He laughed when her mouth dropped open and then he clucked. His horse veered off to the right. "Let's go over here to this stream. There looks to be some rocks to sit upon, grass, trees."

She followed, her heart pounding all the more.

He hopped off and let his horse wander to the stream. Then Mr. Easton reached up to help her down.

The pounding increased. The thought of his hands around her again brought a rush of heat to her face.

"What's this? Smiling and blushing? Some might call you a new debutante."

"Oh, you are too much." Her indignation rose, and she tried to wiggle down without assistance.

"There's no need to be like that. I'm just making light." His hands circled her waist and he lowered her slowly to stand right in front of him. His grin was contagious and close. He smelled of earth and some kind of soap. "I consider that one of the most enjoyable things I've been able to do at this house party."

"Lowering me off my horse."

"Yes." He dipped his head and then stepped away and offered his arm. "Shall we?"

His comments, astounding, one after the other were lingering wreaking havoc on her peace of mind. Her stomach leapt in happy expectation. They made their way to a small area next to the stream. There were several lovely large flat rocks. The two horses found patches of grass.

The sun broke through the clouds again and Oscar chose a rock that was surely warm. He took off his jacket and laid it out. "For you, my lady." With a bow and a flourish of his hands, she thought him as genteel as any man she'd met. And certainly as handsome. With his hair all over his head instead of carefully brushed back, he looked even more so. "You know, you have a roguish look about you."

His own eyebrow rose to match hers. "And does that appeal to you? If so, I admit, I'm surprised to hear it."

"Not really, no, but I'm enjoying this look, nonetheless."

His own mouth dropped open as he sat down beside her. "Just what are you saying?"

The breadth of his shoulders stood out more without his jacket. The muscles in his arms were large and strong.

She swallowed. "I'm just saying that I like this look, with your hair in the wind. It suits you."

"Hm. So the other ladies will like it too? Perhaps I should wear it thus to the ball?"

"No." The word and its abrupt tone came out without her even thinking about it.

He tipped his head to the side, suddenly very amused with everything about her.

She shifted in her seat and cleared her throat. "Will there be a ball?" She had begun to avoid balls. But perhaps for this party, she would make an exception.

"There will be, yes, but likely smaller dances on other evenings as well."

She nodded. "Ah, I would expect as much." She tried to brush the hair out of her face, but her hand got caught in the knots. She must look a sight.

He studied her face. She felt his gaze travel over her skin as if a warm blanket. Though embarrassed by her appearance, she didn't look away.

He reached a hand out to her hair. His fingers moving through it sent waves of sensations over her. "I

wish you would always wear your hair just like this."
He tugged a twig out, gently, the subtle pull against
every hair on her head sending tingles all the way to
her toes.

"You do? Twigs and all?"

"Yes, it's lovely. Especially flowing out behind you on a
horse. I almost didn't want to catch up because the view
was so lovely."

She opened her mouth, but her tongue went dry. She
didn't know what she would say anyway. When had a man
ever thought her lovely?

"May I assist in detangling it for you?" He gathered her
hair behind her head and started running his fingers
through the ends.

Her nod was all she could manage.

"I used to do this for my sister sometimes."

"Tabitha? Well, I mean, Lady Hamilton?"

"Yes. She was always running with us as boys and she
would get in all kinds of scrapes, but mostly her hair after
horse rides would be such a tangled mess she'd cry when
our nursemaid tried to run a brush through it."

"Oh, that's dreadful."

He continued to work through her hair, separating bits
and working on the ends in so gentle a fashion that she
would beg for more if he stopped.

"Yes, so I worked through the worst of it before the
nursemaid got a hold of her."

"That's… that's lovely. This is lovely. You've quite a
talent."

"Hmm." He continued his ministrations. Every part of
her reacted in a delicious warmth. What thought had she
for cold? When had another treated her with such gentle-
ness? With such care? His fingers brushed her neck as he

worked on her knots. A trail of tingles followed, all along the softness of her skin.

"Tell me more of your family." She managed to speak, her words a hoarse whispery sound.

"They're great, really. Edward. Well, he's frustrating me lately. Things have been different since he began to think of marrying. But he and I were best friends growing up. And when Tabitha was born, we sort of united around her. Kept her from… well, from the men you're trying to avoid." He leaned forward to see her face. "When I look at it in that way, I understand a bit more where you're coming from. It was the devil trying to keep Tabitha safe." He chuckled. "And I'm sure she thought it was the devil too."

"But you all approved of Lord Hamilton?"

"Oh, yes. He grew up with us. Our best friend, almost a brother himself." He laughed. "Turns out Tabitha loved him. For all that time." He shrugged. "And we trusted him."

Eva smiled listening to him. "So you trusted him." She nodded. What a lovely thought. Was there anyone in the world she trusted? As she lifted her face up to the sun, aware of every shift of Mr. Easton's body next to her, she suspected she might one day trust him. But…her heart shuddered at the thought. She couldn't love him. Could she? Perhaps time would tell. Now, alone on a rock, with his fingers in her hair, she thought anything was possible. "Your family sounds lovely. I wish I'd had even one sibling."

He pulled her hair back. "This will be better. And for the return ride, perhaps you'd be best to tie it back." He kept adjusting her hair, moving it here and there, as if toying with it and she wished he would never stop.

"Must we ride back so soon?"

He let his fingers run through her hair one more time. "No. Not at all. Just thinking ahead."

She nodded.

When he stopped, she missed his touch immediately. But she did want to see his face. She turned. "Do you miss them? Do you regret not spending Christmas with them all?"

He studied her face. "I'll see them. I'll head straight back and catch Twelfth Night." After a moment, he added. "I don't think I will ever regret coming to this house party." His eyes searched hers. Did he shift closer or had she imagined it?

She sucked in her breath. What was he saying? "So, you're happy I invited you?" She hesitated, almost wishing she hadn't asked, afraid of his answer.

"I've been happier here than I have in a long time." His hand lifted and brushed a hair off her forehead, softly, a caress. His eyes studied her, their pleased enjoyment sending a rush of light through her.

His face was close now, closer all the time. His eyes sparkled at her. His lips were soft-looking. His expression was intent. She leaned closer. Her hand rested on his arm, drawn as though she couldn't resist. He had a row of freckles. They matched his hair. The crinkles of his eyes deepened with the eternal happiness that seemed to hover about him. His mouth quirked up. She wondered what it would be like to press her lips to his, just once. Were they soft? Firm? He dipped his face, his mouth closer, eyes asking.

The energy that lit between them pulled at her, closing the distance further. Thought left, and she closed her eyes, hoping his lips would touch hers, hoping to feel what it was like in his arms, a man she trusted, or hoped to trust.

When his lips brushed hers, the barest touch ignited a roaring surge inside that she did not know what to do with.

She leaned into him, but he stopped. When she opened her eyes his looked... troubled.

"Oh." She paused. "Oh dear."

He held up a finger. "Now, perhaps not *oh dear*."

"How so?" She was still near, her mouth catching the tickles of his breath puffing out. She held back from pressing her lips to his anew. Even though she knew such a thing could never be a good idea.

"I'm a gentleman. We enjoy each other. And how could saying, 'I enjoy you,' be an, 'Oh dear?'"

"I like that. But." She frowned and created more distance.

His gaze immediately keyed in to her lips again. "In fact. I'd like to kiss you again." His boyish grin, the hope in his eyes, made her smile. He lifted a hand and ran his finger down the side of her face. She leaned into him. Then his thumb caressed her mouth. "I do enjoy you." His smile grew. And she could resist no longer. This time, she closed the distance herself and captured the softness of his mouth the way she wished he'd done the first time.

His hands travelled around her back and he held her, loved her, at least that's what it felt like. She melted into him, her lips responding again and again. His softly exploring, asking, and then insisting. Her hands went up around his neck.

He pulled her to her feet, holding her close, up against him.

Her world spun in happiness, everything dancing in a light energy.

And then he paused. He held her close a moment more. "Wow, Lady Evaline. I..." He closed his eyes.

"That was..." She smiled, their lips close enough she could feel his responding smile against her own.

Then she laughed. And he joined her. "I didn't expect that would happen when I woke up this morning." She grinned.

He took her hand in his and led her toward the stream. "Nor I." He looked at her and then away. One hand went through his hair. Was he second guessing their kiss?

A new sort of panic trembled through her, and all her defenses shot up into the sky in a barrier none would ever break through. "I suppose… some would make rash decisions based off a moment like this."

His gaze flit to hers. Was that relief she saw? "Right. Like rush off to talk to your father."

She shook her head. "When nothing like that is necessary. No one is here."

"Your reputation is safe with me."

She nodded. "We already know how much you abhor the idea of marriage." She watched him.

"We do." He nodded again and again as though convincing himself.

"Exactly. But that was… nice."

"Agreed. Remarkable." He paused, searching her face.

She leaned closer. He closed the distance, but she turned away. "Of course, it can never happen again."

"Of course not. When people might see or know."

"Or ever." She stared him down, summoning every ounce of self-control left in her weak and rebellious body. "I'm not accustomed to the ways of some women."

He nodded. "No, of course not. I do not think you are. When I say I planned to behave as a gentleman, I meant every word. There are very few women I have ever kissed." He swallowed. "And none such as you."

"You are the only kiss for me."

His face burned a fascinating red. "In all honesty, you

are my first as well. If you don't count the grade school challenges I accepted when we were young."

She laughed, delighted.

They walked a few more steps in an awkward sort of silence. Oscar seemed to have an air of perfect calm.

How could he be so unaffected? Eva's insides raged. And she knew that she would never, ever, be the same.

Chapter Twelve

✿❀✿

Oscar was aware of every swish of her skirt, of every breath that escaped her mouth. Every turn of her head and every shimmering movement of her magnificent hair all tantalized his every sense. Never again? Never capture those delicious lips again with his own? How could she remain so unaffected? His every thought, every instinct, every inclination was toward her right now, and more than anything he wished to sweep her in his arms and capture her delicious mouth over and over again.

But what would that accomplish? Did he wish to marry the woman? He eyed her again. And shocked himself when an actual consideration to do just that paraded across his mind. Certainly, he would have done his duty by her. But as she'd said, she had no expectation or need for him to rescue her reputation. So now what? Given a choice, after such an experience, for the first time in his life, marriage seemed a pleasant option. More than a pleasant option. A... need? For her? He was astounded by his reaction. And wholly unprepared. He had nothing to offer her. No means. No home, only Edward to provide for them both. He refused to live off her dowry. That was simply not acceptable. Just the idea that any of these thoughts entered his mind was astounding.

He'd never felt so shaken. First the kiss of all kisses and then this new revelation. He needed to sort this through.

She fidgeted. Her face looked drawn and tired and worried.

But first, he needed to be a gentleman. His silence was most certainly disconcerting to her. "I apologize for my woolgathering. I… there is much to think about."

"Might I know the direction of your thoughts?" The flitting passage of fear got his attention. Did she worry that here again was another man smitten by her charm, by the first inclination toward anything friendly and he would fall all over her? He could set her at ease at least in that regard for whether or not he was considering marrying her, he was not ready at this point.

"I was thinking that I can very easily see why many a man would be smitten by the first smiles you send their way."

"You can?" Her eyes widened, the discomfort obvious. All the talk of her turning into Lady Snow as soon as a man showed her any attention rushed through his mind.

He held up his hands. "But you need have no fears concerning me. I know how to keep my perspective clear. I will not be like those hungering after you." Respect. He would show her the respect she deserved.

"I understand." Her face pinched a moment, and she looked away.

"Wait, is this sadness I see?"

She turned again to face him. "Of course not. I... I'm only cold."

"Oh, of course." He jogged back to his jacket they'd left on the rock. "Please wear this."

She already had a warm riding habit, but his jacket fit over the top if it all.

"Thank you." Her voice sounded small to his ears.

"Are you well?"

She nodded.

"Can I get more than a nod? I see the nod, but I feel like perhaps you're not smiling or behaving as you usually would were you to be truly well."

She whipped around to face him. "I'm thinking, as you are. There's a lot to think about. Something big just happened. Perhaps it is nothing to you, but I need time to think about... things."

"It is not nothing..."

She held up her hands. "No need to explain further. I think it just makes things worse."

"Worse..."

"Certainly. Let's just both get through this and then things can be back to normal tomorrow." She choked. "Or soon, perhaps." She looked away.

"Back to normal." He shook his head. She couldn't possibly think anything would ever be *normal* between them again. But her lip quivered, and her hand tensed in his. He released her when more than anything he wanted to pull her into his arms, but he didn't dare. "What can I do?"

"Nothing. Really. Let's walk by this stream a moment and then return to the house. We have a long ride and I'm certain people will notice."

"I asked a few of them to cover for us. And the stable-master as well."

She nodded but didn't seem to be really hearing him.

They walked along in silence a moment more. Then she surprised him by picking up a stick. "Shall we race?" She threw it in the stream, and they watched it float away.

"Certainly." He found one of his own and she another.

They threw sticks for a time, and he should have been grateful for a lightening of the mood. But too many things felt unexplained.

When they finally returned to the house, no one had really noticed their absence. Lady Evaline hurried upstairs, and he plodded along slowly after. But partway up, Mr. Shaw came walking down, so Oscar waited on the stairs. "And it's my dear host. How are you this afternoon?"

"I'm well. I trust you are enjoying our humble house party?"

"Very much, sir. I wonder, might I have a moment of your time? I find I am in much need of guidance."

His kind eyes turned perceptive. "In matters of the heart or finances?"

He wanted to say both. "Finances. I should like to know how to make my own way in the world."

"Excellent. I have a moment right now, if you'll come into my study?"

"Oh, thank you." Oscar turned on the stairs and walked with him back down and then followed him to his study.

"What can I do for you?" he indicated that Oscar should enter through a thick, dark-wood door.

"I'm a second son."

The man chuckled. "I could tell you to say no more, for all your troubles were revealed in that single statement, but I'll hear you out."

"Thank you. Perhaps mine is just like all others. But I would like to change things if possible."

"Most would just say to marry well. You're a good-looking chap. You're young…" He watched Oscar closely, and Oscar chose to answer carefully.

"I wish to offer something to the marriage myself. I feel… it doesn't sit well to live off the income of another."

Mr. Shaw appraised him. "That is very noble of you." He poured two glasses of brandy and offered one to Oscar.

"I'm not as noble as you might think. I cannot abide going to my brother for every increase, for special occasions, for anything anymore."

"And you wish to marry?"

He shifted in his seat. But the man's eyes saw too much. "I do."

"To my grandniece?"

He choked, the burning liquid catching fire in his throat. "Pardon me?"

Mr. Shaw laughed to himself. "I was married twice you know. I have outlived both of them."

"I'm sorry to hear that. About losing two wives. I am most grateful you have lived such a long life."

"Yes, thank you. So now, let's talk. What can I do for you?"

They discussed Oscar's financial situation. He asked Mr. Shaw a great many questions and when their conversation was nearly over, he swirled the liquid in his cup. "So, if you can find investors and get yourself even one ship, you are well on your way to your own source of income. Of course, before that, you could make arrangements with those that do have ships, and invest yourself in their ventures and start turning a profit." He downed the rest of his drink. "But I wouldn't spend it all. You don't need the latest jacket. You don't need more than one equipage, more than a team of horses and one to ride, unless you would buy and sell through Tattersalls, and that would be another manner in which to earn money."

Oscar's mind was racing through all the information he'd just heard. "This is most useful. Thank you. I have a bit saved away. I will immediately begin saving for my own ship. Perhaps, Mr. Shaw, perhaps you shall see me one day and I will have a whole fleet to boast of." Everything he'd just learned filled him with a wild and unique sense of freedom. His smile grew and Mr. Shaw laughed at him. "Enjoyed this whole conversation, didn't you?"

"I did. To be free and unbeholden to anyone is a great blessing, indeed."

"I quite understand. I haven't always had as much as I do now. In fact, I've made quite a bit more in the later years. Most of these guests don't know the half of it. I can tell you as you're not any relation to me, but my wealth is considerable, indeed. I grew most of it through shipping and trade."

Oscar's heart picked up. He was suddenly full of energy. "I shall send out letters today, this very moment. Surely I can find some investors, and I think I will also invest in a few of my own." He eyed Mr. Shaw. "Might I invest in yours?"

The old man's eyes widened. "But of course. I am putting together a new ship right now." He pulled out some papers. "I'll have my solicitor draw up the agreements. We'll get it taken care of here at the party." He eyed him a moment more. "And do let me know what you come up with. Perhaps it might be something I'd like to be involved with as well."

"Thank you. I will." Oscar's mind was already running

through all those he knew, planning to approach shipping companies as well, when Mr. Shaw said something. It took a moment for Oscar to notice he was speaking. "I do apologize. I think my mind is working out the details already."

Mr. Shaw laughed. "Then I'll leave you to it. Feel free to use my study. The ink and parchment is here. If any inheritance seekers come knocking, just send them on their way. But if my niece stops by, feel free to invite her in, but leave the door open." He winked and before Oscar could say another word, he'd left the room.

Once all his correspondence was completed and in the hands of a servant to post, Oscar went in search of a bit of luncheon. Voices in the main dining hall drew him and the happy sight of a buffet full of food made his stomach growl.

"And here he is. Mr. Easton himself." Lord Stanhope waved a hand over. "Come tell us about the phaeton races."

He'd forgotten about them. How odd. He waved and went to fill a plate with food. Upon arriving at the party, some paltry days past, had he really cared principally for an opportunity to participate in the phaeton races? He shook his head. And now, the thought of wasting money on something so frivolous felt foreign. He had a shipping company to begin. And a lady to impress? Lady Evaline's face entered his mind at the most surprising times.

By the time he joined their group, more had gathered and the sound of their voices excitedly picking winners from those racing nearly drowned out all sound. He smiled and welcomed the pats on his back. As he brought the first bite to his mouth, he was suddenly the focus of all their attention. He must have missed something. "Pardon?"

"Aren't you racing? We saw your name on the list."

He choked and then swallowed some of the lite ale.

"Was it? Someone must have enrolled me without my knowing."

"Are you going to race, though? What do you know about the other contenders? We're placing bets."

"Are you?" His grin widened. Here was a way to make some quick blunt. But something Mr. Shaw had said came back into his mind. *"Don't fall prey to the lie of so many of your peers. Cards, gambling, betting on the horses. None of this is a sure way to earn a decent living. You will lose more than you win. Mark my words."*

So, he let the comment pass. After another bite, with eyes still on him, he shrugged. "I don't know, gentlemen. I'll tell you this much. Edward is entering and that man never loses anything."

Their chatter increased between themselves. Oscar smiled. He'd probably just amped up the odds for his brother. But if Oscar were to count on anyone winning, it was Edward. The man didn't know how to lose, at anything. Perhaps he'd want to invest some of his winnings in Oscar's new as yet-to-be-created shipping business.

A conversation to his left caught his attention as if his ears heard every mention of Lady Evaline.

"I heard Lady Snow was out on a horse all morning long. And she wasn't alone."

The base laughter made Oscar's stomach boil.

"Who was the lucky man?"

"No one knows. But if she's warming up to one, she might warm up to any of us."

"I already told you. She smiled at me." Talmus. Oscar wanted to punch Talmus.

Lord Knightsbridge smirked. "Cold or not, I've told you. I'm willing to put up with a lot when the chit has a dowry her size."

Oscar's fists clenched. "Mind your tongue. You speak of a lady I hold in high esteem."

The men in his group and in Talmus' all paused what they were doing. The room grew quiet, but Oscar didn't even care. He waited, his eyes locking with the last man to speak.

"So you're willing to stand up for her honor now, are you?" Talmus sneered. "Care to revise what you keep telling the rest of us? You sure the two of you are just friends?"

"We're friends." He gritted his teeth, and in that moment, wished he could claim her and settle this once and for all.

"Then I don't think you have any place to call any of us out. We're just speculating on the availability of one of the ladies among us."

"I'll have you speak kindly and with respect though, especially in mixed company." Oscar indicated the women at the other end of the table who were also silently paying close attention.

They sat taller and changed their demeanors remarkably quickly. "Beg our pardon. A bit of a joke, that's all." Talmus nodded to the ladies, frowned at Oscar, and then downed the contents in his cup. "I need something stronger than this."

But Oscar's emotions were all on fire. His fists were still clenched and right now, what he wanted, was to place one in the center of their faces. But such violent thoughts surprised him as much as satisfied his anger.

And then Lady Evaline herself entered. She glanced about the room in one swift motion and then moved to the buffet. Oscar willed her to look his direction. When she didn't, he almost stood to help carry her plate, but Talmus started laughing at him. The dolt of a man had both eyebrows raised, and he crossed his arms. What was his point exactly? Oscar might have words with him later.

He kept his eyes on Lady Evaline, but she didn't once look in his direction. Much to his dismay, she moved instead to sit right in the middle of Talmus and his friends.

Oscar wanted to wipe the smug satisfactory smiles off each one of their faces. But instead he had to listen to her laughs and see her smiles, all directed at the scum of the party. Was this what he'd encouraged her to do? To warm up to the other men? He stood with a jerk, his chair tumbling back behind him. Everyone tuned to look again at him. Even Lady Evaline. He nodded once in their direction and turned towards the door.

Chapter Thirteen

Eva was nowhere near ready to see Mr. Easton in any of the public rooms. When she entered for a bite of luncheon, she tried not to see him, tried not to talk to him, tried to sit anywhere but with him. Her face was ablaze, and she was certain every person in the room would know they'd kissed. But she felt his gaze, and she could hardly resist. So instead, she'd done everything she could to forget he was there. Didn't he say he wanted her to be more cordial? She turned her smiles on the nearest group of men, realizing too late that these particular men were her least favorite. Mr. Talmus seemed overly pleased at her choice, and she knew she would regret it later.

As Oscar attempted to leave, a group of ladies at that end of the table called him over. Their giggles and carrying-on sent another entirely new sensation racing through her insides. Was she jealous? She glanced in his direction and his laugh of pure enjoyment sent her fingers digging into her palms. She *was* jealous. So terribly jealous. She could hardly breathe. Everything felt tight. She didn't hear the conversation around her. She ate two bites and then stood to leave.

She hardly heard the men calling their farewells, and then she walked by Mr. Easton without a glance and out the door.

She wanted nothing more than to rage a fiery tempest at someone, but there was nothing for it. No avenue for her anger, nothing to express such a foreign emotion. Jealous of attentions she herself did not welcome? Did she? She yearned for them, wished to once again be in his arms, but was that the same as wanting a courtship? Wanting his time? His attention? His conversations? She assumed so. But how could that be? She most decidedly did not want anything from any man who would then reject her or continue to have feelings for others as well. Mr. Easton with a table full of women was exactly her worry when considering marriage.

The tiniest, far away thought tried to remind her that she and Mr. Easton had no understanding and that he was just doing his duty as a gentleman at the party. But her emotion was too strong to listen to such a placid and weak thought. She huffed through the front hall and was about to make her way to her room to cry off everything for a headache.

Mr. Shaw's voice stopped her. "Oh, Lady Evaline. There you are."

She counted to five. She tried to calm her features. She relaxed her shoulders, and she turned to their dear host. "Uncle." Her smile was sincere. She cared for this man. "How are you today?"

"I'm well. I was particularly impressed with a friend of yours, Mr. Easton."

"Oh?" She knew the coloring in her face was likely changing all shades.

"Yes, he's an impressive fellow, determined to make his way in the world. He has good plans. I wouldn't be surprised if he found the success that I have."

She turned more fully to face him. "You've talked?"

"Yes. I happened upon him in his riding gear, much as I'm happening upon you now. It's amazing how this works. He expressed his desire to earn his living and I got him started on his way. Judging by the pile of correspondence he sent out, I'd say he was serious about things." Mr. Shaw stepped closer and winked. "Perhaps you might know better than I his motivations?"

She sucked in her breath, not sure whether to feel glee or dread or embarrassment. "I'm not certain I understand why I would know anything about his financial affairs, but I think you must be the kindest of men to help him." She smiled, hoping that would be the end of things.

But he only laughed. "Pity you can't see it, for I think every effort he's making now is because of a strong attachment to someone." His eyes twinkled back his meaning, but she refused to acknowledge it.

Even with her dismissal, he continued. "He looked to me like a man who wants to propose, but must first ensure he has something to offer."

Her mouth dried instantly, and words froze in her throat. Her hand went to her chest which had seized.

"But these things take time. So if he doesn't fall down on a knee during the party, take heart. If I'm reading things correctly, he will soon enough, when he feels he deserves you." He patted her arm. "That's just the kind of man I hope all you sweet good girls can find." He turned to walk away. "And he is investing in my shipping, so you can't blame a man for favoring someone so useful to himself." He straightened his jacket as he made his own way toward the luncheon.

She tried to relax any part of her for everything seemed to be tight and strung, but nothing was functioning. Even her legs seemed stiff. Her breathing came faster and faster. She clutched her stomach and the world started to look grey around the edges.

She must not swoon. She was not a swooning type of woman. She would not. She could not. To steady herself, she sat on a stair and pulled her knees up to her chest. They worked as the perfect resting place for her head.

Everything seemed to steady. But she daren't move just yet.

The ladies who'd been doting on Mr. Easton came giggling out of the room. As they passed her without a glance, one laughed. "And he's asked me for the first set. That has to mean something. Imagine. An Easton." They all giggled again. "They are the most handsome brothers in all of the ton, I'm certain of it." The other stood closer and their conversation moved too far away to be heard.

Asked her for the first set? Shouldn't Eva be dancing the first set with him? If he was going to be passing around kisses, first sets should come hand in hand, she imagined. But what did she know of these things. As she'd embarrassingly admitted, she'd never kissed another before. She didn't imagine she would be kissing anyone ever, and yet here she was. She stood and held a hand out on the wall to steady herself. She knew a lovely library to be located just off the stairs to her right, away from where the ladies had gone. She made her way there. When a servant passed, she stopped her. "Could you bring me some tea in this library here? I'm feeling in need of constitution."

"Yes, my lady. If you like I can offer you some of Cook's powders."

"That would be lovely, thank you. Perhaps, two cups?"

The maid bobbed a curtsey, and Eva sat in a comfortable chair by the fire.

The mantle had been dressed. A tree in the rear of the room held garlands and lovely candles, unlit. Berries of red filled the boughs. She felt immediately improved. Her nose welcomed the beautiful smells of pine and burning logs in the fire. She sat at a chair there, leaned back her head and might have fallen asleep.

Her last thoughts, jumbled though they were, involved Lord Thomason and his excuses whenever she asked him about the other ladies he always entertained. At every ball, every public gathering, he would dance with as many ladies as he could. He stood at her side and danced their customary two sets, but every other spare moment, he was entertaining women and flirting. Had he ever flirted with her? Yes, in a way. But never in the more baser ways she'd heard him do with the other women. One time on the way to the receiving room, she'd heard him in a corner with a lady. Her giggles sounded much more intimate than they should, or so she'd thought, but when she approached, his immediate attention had switched wholly to her with compliments and sweetness so she'd let it go. Was she repeating her same error? Falling for a man who didn't know how to love her as she wanted to be loved? That was the crux of it. But did anyone love her? Could anyone?

Though her thoughts had been troubled, she awoke feeling much better. A tray with tea waited on the table in front of her. She felt the side of the pot. Still warm. Making her own tea in a room by herself felt familiar and like home. She stirred the sugar and cream into her tea, sniffed Cook's powders and decided against them, then took her first sip. "Lovely."

When she finally left her small solace, she felt prepared to face the day. People seemed to be gathering in the same room where they played cards.

A nice, older gentleman whom she had spoken little with called her over. "Lady Evaline, just the woman we are needing to come advise us." Mr. Ludwig's smile was warm, his outstretched hand welcome to her ready heart.

"Oh? I'd be pleased to join you."

He sat with three ladies she'd enjoyed her biscuits with. Miss Darlene, Lady Fenning, and Lady Constance. Of all the women here at this house party, these three seemed worthy of friendship. For the first time, she felt an inclination to perhaps participate in a bit of a coze. Mr. Ludwig notwithstanding. She smiled at each.

"We are discussing the impending weather."

She tapped her chin, remembering the clear skies from earlier this afternoon. "Are we expecting some weather?"

"We are." He nodded as decisively as any man. "I feel it in my elbow, just so." He tapped the bend in his arm as though it were the definitive answer to all weather predictions. "It aches in just the way to indicate coming snow."

"Snow?"

The other ladies seemed passively interested.

"Yes, and it is going to be quite a large dropping if my predictions are accurate."

"And how often are your predictions accurate?" Miss Darlene smiled warmly, but there was a hint of concern in her face.

"I'm correct every time." He winced. "Well, except for the wedding of our dear neighbors."

"What happened there?"

"They pushed it back according to my emphatic direction only to find they'd missed the only beautiful sunny day that month. They were married in the most pouring deluge we've had to this date."

Eva nodded. "Then we shall have to see, shan't we?"

"Mark my words. My elbow doesn't lie." He coughed. "Except for that one time."

Lady Fenning pulled out the Whist cards and Eva and Lady Constance teamed up. "I never lose." Lady Constance laughed. "That's a great blessing for us, then, because I think I lose every time."

The others nodded their agreement and Eva wondered if tonight might be one of her very few losses at Whist.

When Mr. Easton entered the room, he caused a significant energy from one table. They called to him in excited giggles, and he stepped in their direction. But he did look across the room toward her. She looked away. There. She could avoid his attentions. She could conquer her feelings. She could go on as before. But before she could lay down a single card, Lady Constance was looking up over Eva's shoulder at something. That's when she felt Mr. Easton's delicious breath on her neck and lovely smell of sandalwood which overpowered whatever senses she had. Suddenly it was all Mr. Easton.

His voice rumbled through her. "I see you're well on your way to continuing your winning streak."

She hugged the cards to her chest. "Mr. Easton." When she turned, his face was close, and full of caring. Had he returned to being simply friendly? That would help things.

She dared show him another peek. "If you see here. It is very likely I may lose this once."

He shook his head. "I will not believe it of you." He lifted his chin to address the table as a whole. "I have it on good authority that she never loses at Whist."

They smiled at him.

"Mr. Easton, we are waiting to begin." The loudest of the original group of ladies waved her hand from their distant table and pouted.

"Who is that?" Eva tried to sound as though she didn't care, but Mr. Easton's amused expression told her she had failed. She recognized the voice somehow.

"That is Miss Penny. And I have it on good authority that she cannot live without me at her side." He winked. Then, before Eva could huff in irritation, he whispered. "I know exactly how she feels, though my sentiments are directed right here at you."

Her face heated and her throat grew tight. She tried desperately to compose herself before she looked up and played the exact opposite card she was meant to. "Oh dear, no. I meant to lay another."

"Too late." Mr. Ludwig chuckled and placed his card, showing Eva just how wrong her choice was. She lost the hand and the game.

The butler entered. He spoke to the room. "If you'll excuse me, a group has gathered. They're singing if you wish to have a listen."

Mr. Easton was behind her before she could attempt to stand, pulling back her chair and offering his arm. "Would you join me?"

"Yes, of course." She placed her hand on his arm and allowed him to lead her from the room.

The beautiful sounds of their blended voices entered

the main hall and echoed up to the ceiling. "Oh, that's lovely."

Miss Penny walked by, her nose a little higher in the air than usual. "Whoever heard of singing hymns outside the church?"

Eva turned to Mr. Easton. "You sing outside the church, don't you?"

He cleared his throat. "I don't, that is to say, the Easton's sing and we carol, but I myself do not do so very well."

"I cannot believe it. Our duet was lovely."

"Your part of our duet was lovely, I'll admit to that. 'Tis true. But whether or not I add anything to the group, I always sing this time of year. It is not Christmas unless every Easton man is singing, says my mother. May she rest in peace."

"I'm sorry she is no longer here."

"Oh, she's here alright, about the place. She's haunting me if I don't do my duty at Christmastime and sing."

He was so cheery, so sincere, she found herself quite at ease. Her hand fit comfortably on his arm, her body closer to his side. The carolers began their next song, "Adeste Fideles," one of her favorites. "Oh this is wonderful." She swayed at his side. And then Mr. Shaw joined in. "Come now. Everyone." He raised his hand.

And they all joined. At first Mr. Easton's singing could hardly be called such. It was more lip movement and a soft murmur, but when he found her looking and trying to listen, he shook his head with a big smile and began to sing out his notes. He was passably good, but he sang with such gusto, the Latin words flowing easily from his lips with such happiness, that those around merely smiled larger. They sang several more and when they finished the "Holly and the Ivy," the group of carolers all bowed or curtseyed to Mr. Shaw. "God bless all in the Ivy Manor."

"God bless. Please come in. Our cook's brewed up some of her delicious wassail."

The servants had brought out tables and big vats of wassail. They were scooping out cups for one and all. Oscar immediately left to get two cups for them. She knew she was in trouble, indeed. For his presence was immediately missed. Could she not stand alone amongst all these carolers? Could she not enjoy the festivities without him at her side? It appeared not. Not without wishing for him. She counted the moments until he returned.

Chapter Fourteen

Oscar had watched Eva fill with light as she sang, her voice, pure music. She knew every word, sang every note. When Mr. Shaw asked if any would like to join the carolers, Oscar knew he'd best volunteer the two of them. And he was rewarded. Her smile filled her face. "Oh, would you like to, really?" She turned to him, both hands on his arm, face lifted in happiness.

"Of course. You heard me. I'm a natural." The hand he placed over hers was noticed. Her expressions changed immediately to supreme appreciation.

And then she laughed, the sound almost as musical as her singing.

"You love to sing." He grinned.

"That I do. If you don't mind my sounds, I love to make them."

"What I love best is watching your face when you sing." He laughed. That's what he loved best about everything she did.

146

"Dare I admit that I too like watching you sing?" Her face colored and he found her charming.

"You may admit any such things of that nature. I'll keep them with me when I am alone to nudge a smile to return to my face."

"I imagine you are always smiling."

"Not always. But I do admit that caroling has proved more enjoyable than I thought. I wish we'd seen more when I was a lad."

Eva began in a burst, almost jumping to her toes. The words tumbled out. "I have to tell you a funny story. When I was little, perhaps ten years old, the mummers came by."

"Those mangy-looking folks who sing for money?"

"Yes, except mangy-looking isn't what I would call them. Where I live, they were perfectly lovely, though perhaps a bit threadbare. I loved their singing so much I gave them my entire allowance and then snuck outside and sang with them for miles."

"You didn't." Though he could very well imagine she did.

"Certainly, and I was naturally severely punished." She brushed hair from her eyes that he had been longing to touch. "But it was worth any punishment. I walked between them and we sung every hymn more than once. Their songs reached the stars I'm certain of it."

"Oh? And what did a severe punishment look like when you were young?"

"No dessert, at all, for two weeks."

"The horror."

"Truth. Even Cook was forbidden to sneak me things."

"But she did anyway."

"Of course. How did you know?"

"Because I have a cook like that. I miss her most of all."

His heart ached for a moment and it came on so suddenly he was unprepared. "She's like a mother to me, especially now that mine's gone."

"Tell me about her."

"She can read me. If I walk in the kitchen, she knows something. As a lad, I avoided her when I'd done something wrong."

She laughed.

"And she sought me out because of it."

"That's incredible. How nice to be noticed and loved." Her eyes filled with the sort of longing he'd never seen or felt. He wished to fill any of her empty spots, to fill them with love and goodness and caring.

Her gaze turned concerned. "Do you wish you were there? With them?"

"No. Not at all. I'll catch Twelfth Night anyway." A sad sort of dull ache joined the already present hole meant for Cook, and he knew they needed to talk about something else or he'd ruin caroling. "I will miss you, when I go. Then there will be a sadness on that end of things. So I'm doomed with this smallish growing hole right here." He pounded his chest with his fist. "I suppose I shall have to learn to endure." He turned most sincere eyes down to her. "Thank you for inviting me." He watched her face. But she didn't close off and she didn't look uncomfortable.

"I will miss you too." Her lashes lifted and she looked deeply into his eyes. There were questions there. Questions he would love to answer if he only knew what they were, precisely. She was a puzzle, this Lady Evaline, a puzzle with a growing hold on his heart.

They sipped their wassail. Lady Evaline's maid arrived with some warmer outerwear, and when she put on a bright red cloak, earmuffs and a muff for her hands, she was the picture of Christmas. Add her rosy cheeks and it all seemed to beckon Father Christmas himself. When had Oscar become so poetic in his thoughts? Certainly never until now. Tabitha might be proud. Edward would laugh, but his mother would have loved it. He donned a large overcoat and hat.

When everyone was ready, they followed the group out the door, heading in the direction of Mr. Shaw's nearest neighbors.

Oscar stepped closer, and she wrapped her arms around his, connecting again with her muff. "This is nice. We'll stay warm."

"I will certainly. You seem to have that effect on me."

She gasped. "Have you no shame?"

"What? I'm being perfectly serious. Take it how you will. I'm always warm when we're together."

She looked over her shoulder. "Perhaps you could keep your voice down, then?"

He glanced around. No one was paying them a bit of mind. "If you like." He leaned closer and nearly kissed her ear as he whispered, "I can think of something I know will warm me up right away if we get cold."

"You did not just say that." Her face heated and she loosened her scarf. "I see what you mean."

He tipped his head back and laughed. "You, my dear Lady Evaline, are a delight."

"Please, call me Eva."

"Eva?" He tilted his head to the side.

"Yes, I demand it of those closest to me."

"Excellent. Eva it is. Though Lady Evaline sounds much more formidable."

She shrugged. "I don't wish to be formidable with you."

That was excellent news as far as Oscar was concerned.

Perhaps she would be open to him progressing somewhat in a courtship with her? Truth is, he'd enjoy getting to know her, calling on her, seeing if they would suit.

"So, Eva." He tried it out on his tongue. "What should we sing next?"

"Oh, I'm certain they've already picked out the music."

And sure as she was standing at his side, they all began singing "While Shepherds Watched Their Flocks." They arrived at the neighbors', but this time no one entered for wassail. The night continued in a lovely manner. Oscar thought it would never be more magical until a soft snow started falling all around them.

"Would you look at that." Eva lifted her hands up out of her muff, tore off her gloves and tried to catch a flake.

He joined with her and showed her the flakes resting on the arm of his coat. Then before she replaced her glove, he took her hand in his, caressing her palm before placing his lips on her knuckles.

She swallowed twice before gifting him a knowing smile and then she put on her glove and hid her hand inside the muff.

The group arrived back at Ivy Manor and sang one last song. The others came out to hear again. It was one of Oscar's personal favorites. He'd really only sung it in church before, but this group seemed well practiced and included harmony to make it even more special. He sang out with his heart, not a care in the world, along with everyone else. They got to verse four and he started to feel something inside, something important. He analyzed his life, his feelings for Eva, his family, Edward's job as head of the family, and Oscar knew that he could do better. He could do better about a lot of things. Making his own living would be a great start. He put his arm around Eva. She leaned her head against him, and they sang together the verse that touched him most.

O ye heights of Heav'n adore him;
Angel hosts, his praises sing;
All dominions, bow before him
And extol our God and King;
Let no tongue on earth be silent,
Ev'ry voice in concert ring,
Evermore and evermore!

He sang the last *evermore* as though he were singing his own praises to the heavens, promising to change, to be better, to do good by this lovely lady under his arm, to have something special to offer her as a husband. He sucked in a breath and nearly choked out a lung. *Her husband.* He dare not look into her face lest she see the words written across his forehead.

He was going to propose to Lady Evaline. To Eva.

His breath was ragged, but his smile grew. And he was going to be the happiest man alive. Even more so than Tabitha's husband Henry, if such a thing were possible.

He squeezed her extra tight, pulling her as close as he dared, and then offered her his arm again. Things were different for him now. But he was not ready. Dash his youth, dash the years he spent moaning about being the second son instead of making something of himself. Dash it all. Because he would ask Eva right now to marry him if he felt ready, if he thought she would say yes. When he led her into the house, Talmus and his group stood on the stairs to welcome them. Their overly large grins made him feel as though he were on a stage to be gawked at. it was as if a magical veil had been lifted. And everything returned to normal. Eva looked up with a worried expression.

"What is it?"

"Nothing. That was my favorite part of this house party yet."

"Mine too, certainly." But Oscar suspected he knew why she looked so concerned and had no way to bring back the lovely magic from a moment before.

"And now we have the special ornament memory tree." The housekeeper called them into a more formal sitting room. At the back of the room was the tallest tree Oscar had ever seen. It reached almost to the ceiling. He'd never seen such a thing. He'd obviously heard of the Queen and the royal household and many of the members of the ton having Christmas trees, but never had he seen one such as the one in front of him. Candles were lit from the bottom to the top. Garlands of berries wrapped around and around so that each bough was covered. Ornaments hung in all colors. All made with the greatest care, he could see they were priceless to the owner. The whole of it seemed magical and beautiful and determined then and there to do something similar with his family. He stood closer to Eva.

Her questioning eyes searched his face but he just shrugged.

They gathered around in front of the glorious tree, and Mr. Shaw stood to talk. "I am so happy to have all of you here. Many of you know I cannot live forever. And I wanted to share at least this one Christmas with almost all my loved ones close." He smiled. "Now we will participate in one of my favorite traditions. For years we would place each of these ornaments on the tree, sharing a memory we have associated with the ornament. They were all made or purchased for a reason. And we've had many a meaningful season because of it."

A pleased murmur moved through the party and Oscar

hoped the guests would help bring cheer to their host's Christmas memories.

"But now, I can't remember all the stories, and you were not here for many of them, so let's play a fun game. If you have a memory with me or the estate, feel free to share it; I would most appreciate it. The housekeeper will be taking notes to help me remember. But if you don't have a memory, share one of your own, or make one up." He laughed. "We will never know."

Everyone seemed excited, if judging by the continued murmur going through the room. Mr. Shaw held up an ornament. "I will begin. One of my earliest memories was my father, having a little chat. He put me on his knee and he said, son, you are the second son. You are not my heir. But I love you still. I'd like to give you a start, but that's all it will be. Don't squander your living. Use it wisely to grow more."

He laughed. "I didn't know what he was talking about at the time, but I took that counsel to heart and when it came time for me to receive my small start, I did as he said. I carefully invested. I started my own ventures. I created relationships with people I wanted to work with. And lo and behold, over time, the money began to grow." His smile grew. "Now it is someone else's turn." He sat.

One by one, people got up to share their memories. Mrs. Widget surprised him and apparently Eva as well, judging by her soft gasp. "I would like to share a memory of a gift sent by Mr. Shaw. My first Christmas without the Mr. I received a lovely shawl in the mail. He said he was thinking of me and knew that Mr. Widget always gifted me a new shawl." She wiped her eyes. "Thank you."

He stood and embraced her and patted her hands until they both sat again.

A few more stood, motivated by her memory to remember similar instances of his kindness, until they were almost finished, judging by the lateness of the hour and the long burning candles.

Eva stood. "I have a few memories with you, dear Uncle. But what I want to share is very recent. From this very house party. I've had three memories I will cherish forever. The first, was visiting with your dear tenants. Thank you for that. The second, riding out across your property on a beautiful mare named Magic. The freedom of that day and all that came with it will stay with me forever." She glanced at Oscar, and he couldn't look away. What was she saying? Had she changed in her desire to be married? Perhaps? "And the third, was tonight. The caroling and the beautiful peace that came from singing the hymns of Christmas." She stepped to her uncle, kissed his cheek, whispering something and then took her seat next to Oscar again.

He put his arm on the back of her chair. "That was nice." He almost kissed the top of her head. Glancing around, he took a deep breath, relieved he hadn't. She didn't seem to have noticed either. He felt so close to her. After their kiss, and caroling, worrying after her, and defending her to the other men, he knew he cared for her. She was important to him. And at the moment felt far more familiar to him than he thought wise to share with the others.

After several others had taken their turn speaking of memories and placing their ornaments, Mr. Shaw stood once more. "And now, we're going to bid you goodnight." Mr. Shaw walked out of the room, everyone waving as he went.

The housekeeper stepped back up to the front of the

room. "You are free to play games, linger, do as you like for the rest of the evening. However, I have an announcement to make before you retire. Tonight while you are sleeping, the servants have been instructed to hang mistletoe in unexpected places."

The squeals from Miss Penny and her friends sounded ridiculous to Oscar's ears, but he couldn't help wonder if Eva felt the same. Would they get another kiss?

The women turned to him and talked energetically to each other. He smiled and then turned away. He'd have to be sure to look over his head before he stalled anywhere in the house.

"Planning how many women you might get to kiss?" Eva adjusted her hands on his arm.

Oscar laughed until he looked at Eva's face and saw she wasn't kidding.

"What? Of course not. I was planning how to avoid some women and how to get trapped beneath more than one bunch with one woman."

She seemed slightly mollified but suddenly, certainly didn't trust him. He'd have to fix that, if he could. Proving himself to her, becoming worthy of her, two new goals that had never previously been a part of his thoughts. Now, these two pursuits motivated and inspired all else in his life. As he watched her charming pink glow and the wonder with which she stared up at the tree, he knew it would be worth every effort.

Chapter Fifteen

✦❦✦

Eva found sleep at last in the wee hours of the morning. Then she awoke, troubled, her stomach in knots. Once dressed, she paced. She'd had a tray for breakfast in her room. The space was small, but sufficed. Back and forth she moved, wringing her hands. "I'm falling in love with Mr. Easton." As soon as the words left her lips, she cringed back from them, from herself. "No. I am not." Her pacing continued. "Yes I am."

She shook her head as she paced. Whatever was happening with her heart and her desires and his attention, it must not, could not be love. And even if it was, she could not allow it. She would tamp it out. Distract herself. Avoid him? She'd tried all those things. Nothing but leaving the party altogether would stop this unexpected turn.

Falling in love meant broken hearts. And he'd given her no reason to think he was any different from any other man, from Lord Thomason. She squinted her eyes tight, trying to erase his memory, but interestingly, as the moment of his betrayal came back into her mind as it had so often, the feelings were dull. She could face the images head on and not cower away. She hadn't loved Lord Thomason. Perhaps long ago she'd thought it love, but all these years, all this disappointment, was based on the mildest of feelings. For nothing she felt for Lord Thomason could even compare to the raging torrent she felt for Mr. Easton.

Dare she leave? "Remy."

"Yes, my lady?" Her maid appeared in the doorway to her closet and bed as though waiting to be called upon.

"I… I don't know what I need."

Remy waited as patiently as ever.

"We might be leaving."

The slight widening of her eyes was the only indication of surprise.

"I think it might be best. But I don't know if I can bear it." The last two words came out as sort of a strangled cry for help.

Remy was immediately at her side. Her one hand on Eva's shoulder gave her a hefty dose of support. For a moment, Eva let the strength of another fill her with courage. She patted her dear servant's hand and nodded her head. "Perhaps be aware that we might leave, at a moment's notice."

Remy nodded. "Yes, my lady."

Eva had no desire to attend church services, but she knew that the days she least desired it, church would most benefit. Or so her governess had told her time and again. Remy helped her dress in her most nondescript dress, which still included delightful swirls of brighter embroidery over the whole of the bodice. She wore her red cloak and carried her muff.

The organ at the front of the lovely church played soft Christmas hymns, many they had sung last night. She made her way to the front. She always sat in the fourth pew from the front. But she stopped. That pew was for a specific family in the area, of course, just as hers was for her family back home. She turned, unsure where to go. Everyone seemed lost in conversation with each other. None seemed to notice her. She walked back a few more rows. Then a hand reached out into the aisle. She looked up. A young man with thick black hair and the sharpest blue eyes she'd ever seen smiled at her and gestured that she sit beside him. He moved to give her the space right by the aisle.

"Thank you."

"But of course. I count myself twice blessed."

"Twice?"

"Yes, I will have company during the service, and my company is of the loveliest kind." He grinned.

She took her hands out of her muff.

"May I?" He held out his hand. "This is very soft. Is it fur?"

"Yes, I think so. You can put your hand inside."

He did. "Very warm indeed, like an oven."

She laughed, remembering Mr. Easton's advice to try to be more kind, warmer. She braved an introduction. "I know this isn't usually done, but if we're to share a pew at church, I'd like to know your name. I'm Lady Evaline."

"Chapman?" His grin grew. "I'm Mr. Lawrence. I grew up near you. We had an estate in the neighboring village, Hampstead."

"Did you?" She studied him. Nothing familiar nudged her memory.

"I was not often at home. Boarding school for my

younger years, then of course Eton and Cambridge." He shrugged. "But the country is the finest in the world." He settled back in their pew. "Though this countryside is stunning on its own. Have you seen much?"

"A bit. I was out on a horse and of course the carriage when we arrived."

"Are you by chance... could I be so fortunate? Are you here at Mr. Shaw's house party?"

"I am, are you?"

"Just arrived this morning."

"Goodness and here you are at church."

"Well, my mother always said, if you don't feel like going, then you most need to attend."

She smiled.

He studied her. "What may I ask brings this smile?"

"I was thinking the very same as I left this morning. How are you related to Mr. Shaw?"

"I'm not. He's just a good soul who taught me everything I know."

She nodded. "It seems he does this for many."

"A brilliant mentor. I've come really just to say thank you, in case... well, he's not going anywhere, is he? Looks healthy as can be."

"He certainly does. I just think perhaps he wanted one more chance with everyone together. If he calls it his last house party, more are likely to come, aren't they?"

"I can see your point. And I'm much relieved he is well."

As the service began, Eva recognized that she felt much better than she had when she awoke. Was it the kindness of this gentleman? Being here at church? The lovely hymns? Whatever the cause, she felt more in control of her emotion. The stained glass at the front depicted Mary and Jesus and the manger. And she thought that especially appropriate as this was the week of Christmas, was it not? Stained glass lined the sides of the church as well, and through one side, sun streamed in, giving everything a colorful glow. Peace filled the room, and a great holiness calmed her heart. Eyes seemed to stare into the back of her head. She tried to ignore them but couldn't and peeked back over her shoulder.

There was Mr. Easton.

He was intent, serious, staring from four rows back. Penny leaned her head closer to Mr. Easton so that she entered Eva's line of sight. Nothing of interest there. Eva return her gaze to the front, a new irritation stirring her peace of only moments before.

Mr. Lawrence gave her a questioning look, but she just shrugged and focused all of her attention on the sermon. What was the pastor saying? Whatever it was, it would wipe out the thought of Miss Penny back there, her claws into Mr. Easton arm, her head near his shoulder. She ground her teeth.

After church, Mr. Lawrence offered his arm and escorted her back to the estate. They ate a lovely luncheon together and sat, pleasantly satisfied for long after, until he stood. "I must attend to some matters of business with Mr. Shaw, but I understand we are to have a ball?"

"Yes, the night before we leave."

"Would you do me the honor of dancing the first set?"

She hesitated only a moment, thinking of Mr. Easton. If she hadn't heard from Miss Penny that his first was taken, she might have suggested the second. "I would love that. Thank you."

"Perhaps the supper set as well?" He lifted one eyebrow,

and she decided he was charming but in no way a danger to her. Her heart picked up on a single beat looking into his handsome face.

"It might be taken. Perhaps ask again?"

"You hold it in reserve?"

The pink of her cheeks gave her away but there was nothing for it. "I'm not sure. I might."

"Is he worthy of such a distinction?"

She tilted her head, studying her hands. "Perhaps." She leaned forward, making a sudden brash decision. "Sometimes, Mr. Lawrence. Sometimes worthiness isn't the issue. It's courage."

His kindly eyes studied her for a moment more. "I believe there is a story there, one that might not have a happy ending for me."

"One can never know the ending until we are upon it."

"Too true, or what would life be, but a marionette performance." He stood taller. "But with freedom and the unknown come risks. What is helpful to ask, no doubt, would be, 'Is he worth it?'"

She sucked in her breath, then nodded.

He bowed to her. "Shall I see you for games later?"

"Of course."

Her gaze drifted. Snow fell in great blankets from her view out the window; it looked as though guests would have a hard time traveling. If she wanted to run away, she'd better do it now. She tried to feel some energy for the idea, to salvage what had been captured of her heart. But instead she watched the big flakes fall in a hypnotic rhythm-less wonder.

Mr. Lawrence returned. "Excuse me."

She stood.

"Oh, no, I did not mean to disturb you." He stepped closer. "My cane."

"Oh, of course." She curtseyed.

He reached for her hand. "But now I may respectfully depart with the promise of games and I just heard, dancing this evening?"

"Excellent."

His lips pressed to her gloved hand, and she wondered at the lack of any feeling in her hand. If he were Mr. Easton, her arm would be set afire with emotion. But she smiled. She was grateful to this nice guest who'd set a very troubled heart at ease.

"Thank you." Her smile was heartfelt.

He lifted his head from a bow and caught her eyes. "You are more than welcome."

"What's this?" Mr. Easton stood in the doorway, a frown not only on his lips but seeming to define his face.

She gasped. Then chided herself.

"Hello, Mr. Easton. This is Mr. Lawrence, Mr. Easton."

Mr. Lawrence bowed low while Mr. Easton barely nodded.

When her new friend turned to her, he winked. "Ah, I see. I'll perhaps meet you later?"

"Yes."

He bowed to them both and left the room.

"A friend of yours?" Mr. Easton entered and sat beside her.

"Yes, a new friend." She didn't love his tone or the manner in which she felt she had to answer for her behavior. "I wonder if he knows Miss Penny and her friends."

His eyes darted to her face and then narrowed a moment before softening. "You know there's nothing there between me and Miss Penny."

"How do I know it?"

"How could there be?" He paused as if he expected her to answer. "Even the thought that someone could be interested in the likes of Miss Penny... it would make most laugh."

"Not most." She looked away, suddenly tired of the conversation.

"There will never be a Miss Penny for me."

Her gaze flit back to his face. The intense gaze caught her eyes. She searched, she challenged, she tried to look away, but she could not, and for a moment, she thought she might believe him. "I would hope not." That's all she could say, all her emotion would allow without the beginnings of an emotional waterfall.

But he seemed to understand. He looked out the door where Mr. Lawrence had just stood. "I'm doing everything I can to prepare. To make myself trustworthy. To be what you might need."

She stood. "Mr. Easton. You are so bold."

"I know. I cannot help myself. Please sit."

She did, wishing he would stop at the same time wishing he would never stop.

"I know you aren't ready to hear words such as these, but I have to wonder, when will you be?"

Her vision blurred. "I don't know."

He turned to stare out at the snow. "Then I will wait."

A great warmth filled the air between them. She recognized it as the peace that came whenever she thought of being with Mr. Easton. Could she grab hold of that peace? Trust it? Trust him? Perhaps. She reached across the arm of her chair, seeking his hand. He laced their fingers together and smiled. "I will wait."

Even though she still knew very little about her own

feelings or desires, this moment felt important and right with the world. But that didn't make it any easier on her heart. The closer she felt to right about another, the more risk she would break her heart. She knew it, and yet she was persisting in this course.

Chapter Sixteen

Two days passed, and Oscar saw little of Eva. She spent much of Monday in her room. He heard tell of a headache. Then the following day, the world thick with snow, she and Mr. Lawrence had been paired together for a sledging. Their laughter carried out across the lawn. Her beauty accentuated by the happiness and ease she must feel with Mr. Lawrence. His one conciliation in the prolonged frustration had been a singular smile sent in his direction when she'd caught sight of him earlier. He's been paired with Miss Penny. The clutching of her hands, the pretend screams as they moved along over the snow were more than he could endure. But she seemed to think that the activity had brought them closer together. On their last ride down the hill, she'd tumbled out, calling out for help with her ankle. He'd no choice but to lift her in his arms and carry her back to the house. Cook had taken over and the family physician called. He'd pronounced her healed. But not until after Oscar had been called upon to read to her in the front parlor while others came in and out to wish their condolences.

Once that had been sorted, he'd gone in search of Eva. Oscar knew Eva cared for him, but she was also having some serious fears about trusting him or any man. She'd been avoiding marriage and pushing away men for years now. And he knew it had something to do with the man she had been engaged to.

But Oscar wasn't ready to take care of a wife. He had to get some things settled first. He was waiting on correspondence from the investors he'd reached out to and also from his solicitor. So many steps and some time stood in his way of an immediate wedding, but he wanted her to know he was there. He wanted to explore a courtship. And he certainly didn't want her to agree to court another while he was trying to get his affairs in order. But how to communicate all of these desires without scaring her or creating some sort of panic about her ridiculous idea that she would never marry. He was certain it wasn't ridiculous in her mind, but to him, nothing could be more foolhardy than an active desire to prevent one's own happiness.

He cared for her. He stopped short of love in his thoughts. Why? Did he love her? What did he know of love? His sister, Tabitha, had loved Henry most of her life. Their love felt natural and long-lived from his perspective. He'd known Eva for but a few days comparatively, months really. But he knew he needed to make some kind of declaration before someone else did. Eva and this new Mr. Lawrence had concerned him. She looked natural and relaxed, something he hadn't seen in her with any other man, besides himself.

The house party would end. How did he know when he would see her again? She didn't seem like one who would participate in the Season or in many of the same house parties he attended. He didn't even know if she had a residence in London.

It was now or never, and he was living in the now. They were to have a sort of on the spot country dance this evening. With the snow, everyone was getting stir crazy, including himself. Who knew what these other men were liable to do or declare.

He had his own problems with others at the party. Eva didn't know, but since their sledging, Miss Penny had been finding him in the most clever hiding places. He wasn't certain how she managed, but he had taken to sitting in his room or staying in highly populated areas of the party just to be sure they wouldn't be caught alone. At the moment, he thought himself well and truly hidden, but the sound of her laughter from down the hallway brought him to his feet.

Outside. Surely she would not follow him outside. He exited a side servants' entrance to be outside for some air and, if he were being honest, to find Eva, and saw that he was completely alone. He circled back along the house, attempting to soak in the sun, the glistening snow, but no sign of Eva only brought further frustration. But no Miss Penny either and that was indeed good news. He didn't hear noise of anyone else and so he meandered along toward the gardens on the side of the house. The servants had worked to create a system of paths. The shrubs all around were still covered in feet of snow, but the sun was out, the paths were clear, and the crisp air felt energizing. He'd received one response to date about his inquiries, a positive one indeed. If things kept progressing, he'd be joining shipping ventures in the early part of next year.

Deep in thought, he jumped when a thump hit his back. "What?" He whipped around but saw no one. He waited. A small giggle made him grin. "Oscar? Is that you?" He thought it must be a rascally young lad relation to Mr. Shaw.

"No!" A young voice called to him from the other side of a hedge.

It most obviously was. "Oh, then who am I fighting?"

"A pirate!"

"Most excellent. I shall fight you, rascally pirate, with snow!" He scooped up a handful and pressed it together.

A bob of hair popped up behind a hedge.

"And you shall walk the plank!" Oscar crept closer, but the hair ran further back into the hedges. He picked up his pace, chasing after him. "I shall throw you in the brig!"

"No, you shan't." A ball of snow careened toward him but missed entirely.

"Ha ha!" He moved toward the origin of the snowball.

The boy ran until he was heaving, sounds of his gasping for air kept Oscar aware of his location. And Oscar wasn't doing any better. They'd circled forward and backward through the hedges until Oscar wasn't entirely certain which was the exit. But the boy finally poked his head out for long enough.

Oscar sent a snowball at him, smacking him in the shoulder. "Aha!"

"You got me!" He grabbed his arm, swayed, and then fell to the snow.

Oscar rushed to him to be certain he wasn't really hurting and then rose an arm and fist in the air. "The winner against Pirate Oscar!"

He sat up. "You know, 'Pirate Oscar,' that has a nice ring to it."

"It does, doesn't it?"

Oscar considered the lad. "I don't think I've ever seen

you outside the nursery." He looked around. "Where is your nursemaid, tutor, or governess?"

"Governess? Why would I need a governess?"

"Well, where are they then? The people who look after you?"

He shrugged.

"Do they know where you are?"

He shrugged again.

Oscar took pity on the lad. "Did you just really want to see all this snow?"

"I did!" His face lit. "None of them can countenance it. They say it's too cold, and I'll catch some sort of every illness known to our household. But I'm out and I was yesterday as well! I haven't caught even a sniffle."

"Very good." He nodded. "Shall we head back to the house then? Just to give them an opportunity to see you're with me and to let you stay out here, perhaps?"

"Do you think that's what'll happen?" The skeptical squint he sent at Oscar gave him pause. But then he shrugged. "We can only try it and see."

"All right then." Oscar trudged along. Oscar smiled. He well remembered feeling just as Oscar appeared to feel now.

When they were closer to the garden exit, the house in full view, a loud friendly shrieking kind of voice called out, "Mr. Easton. There you are." Miss Penny trumped through the snow, cutting across the paths to get to them sooner. "Oh, and if it isn't the most adorable nephew I've ever had!"

Oscar and Oscar both groaned and then shared a look.

She crouched down beside Oscar and squeezed his cheeks and made such a to-do over him that Oscar himself wanted to squirm away.

Oscar searched the paths behind Miss Penny. "Where are the others? Are you out here alone?" He tried to back away from her but hit the edge of a hedge.

She stood. And then reached down for his hand, moving her fingers up his arm to claim a spot near his elbow. "I am. I saw you out the window and wondered if we might take this time for a moment alone." Her gaze, staring meaningfully up into his face, could not be mistaken for anything merely friendly.

"I'll see you later, Mr. Easton!" The scamp ran off before Oscar could help him find his nursemaid.

He lifted his arm and tried to free his hand from Miss Penny, but she clung to him, stepping closer, practically embracing his arm.

Oscar cleared his throat. "I was just on my way in."

"Oh, no you mustn't yet. There's nothing going on in there. We're cooped up and everyone is restless. It's glorious outside, is it not?"

He had to admit it was. Which was why he'd come out in the first place. And to find Eva. He said nothing, but begin a rapid pace back in the direction of the house where they might encounter more people.

Miss Penny kept up, which was appreciated. "I was thinking about how lovely it's been meeting you."

"Oh?"

"Well, yes, we've really had a good time of it, don't you agree? With your sense of humor and mine and our general understanding about most topics, I just cannot imagine feeling more comfortable around anyone else. Some might say that an older plain kind of woman, with say a huge dowry, might be able to keep you company all your days, but she's not the only one at this party with a comfortable living, and some of us are young enough to have only had one Season, you know." She batted her eyelashes.

He almost groaned. The wiles of women were something he could at times not even keep up with. "I'm not certain to whom you are referring on any count. But perhaps you haven't heard. I'm really not looking for marriage at the moment."

"But you are obviously courting Lady Evaline. I cannot understand why." She held a hand to her mouth. "I'm sorry. I don't mean that in any unkind way. It is just that when two people are just so obviously not suited, one has to wonder."

He dislodged his arm at last, wishing to have nothing more to do with her. "My suitability or unsuitability with anyone couldn't be further from your affair. Now, if you'll excuse me. Our private conversation is at an end."

"Oh, but wait. Don't be offended. I just merely meant to point out that you have other options. Right here in front of you."

"I'm well aware. Perhaps you are not aware that I am acting in the manner most designed for my happiness. And if I'm not actively pursuing you, it is not out of ignorance but an informed decision on my part."

Her lip jutted out, but he crossed his arms. And she stepped away in what appeared to be defeat. He could only be grateful. He straightened his waistcoat, ready to depart from her presence, but then she turned and flung herself at him, tripping on the way.

"Miss Penny, what's come over you?"

He caught her as she fell into his arms, her hands clutching at his chest. He eased her balance and set her up on her own two feet again. Then he peeled her hands from his chest but they clung to his arms. "Mr. Easton. Thank you. It's men like you who make this world a better place." Her wide eyes looked up into his face as she stepped closer and ran her hands back up his chest. He couldn't help but laugh.

"Thank you. Now, Miss Penny. Please go show your attention to someone who will appreciate it. I know for a fact that the new Mr. Lawrence is quite a good catch."

She sniffed. "He is enamored with your Lady Evaline."

He started to step back, but froze. "He is?" All of a sudden even more irritated with the situation, he leaned closer to ask her just how she would know such a thing, when Eva herself came around the bend of the house. Her eyes widened. And Miss Penny stepped closer.

"Desist, woman." Oscar pushed her away.

But Eva frowned and then turned back to make her way around the house.

"Well, I can't imagine what's got her all in a huff," Miss Penny started.

"Oh stop, please, Miss Penny." He ran after Eva. But when he rounded the bend, she was nowhere in sight. There were two servants' entrances and a small copse of trees where she could have hidden. The stables were within a reasonable distance as well. His hands shook until he fisted them. She had to hate him, or perhaps he'd ruined her trust and she was devastated. Or perhaps merely tired of him and done entertaining thoughts of him. He couldn't be certain which negative emotion ruled the day. He didn't know, because he couldn't find her.

Chapter Seventeen

❧❧❧

Eva peeked out from the barn door at Mr. Easton as he searched for her. "Don't come in here. Don't. Come in."

"Hiding from someone?" Mr. Lawrence stepped up behind her, and she screamed and then almost collapsed into his arms. Praise everything she hadn't. Because that would have been the least helpful for her knot of emotions.

"Oh, Mr. Lawrence. Hello." She smoothed out her skirts and pulled her cloak tighter around herself. "What are you doing here?"

"I was…tending to my horse. Are you well? You seemed deeply disturbed…" He peered out the crack. "Would you feel better if I told you he'd gone back inside?"

"Oh, thank heavens." She placed a hand on her heart and then frowned. "But that is not your affair."

"Then I'm sorry to say he hasn't gone in but is about to join us." Mr. Lawrence's face was full of apology. "He has changed direction multiple times but is now firmly on his way to the barn."

"No!" She wasn't feeling forgiving.

"Eva." Mr. Easton stepped into the barn. His eyes full of sorrow which only irritated her further.

"Don't call me that."

"Lady Evaline."

"Don't call me that either." She put her hands on her hips and stepped closer to Mr. Lawrence.

Oscar looked from one to the other, his expression growing more desperate. "What you just saw... I know you're sensitive about this particular thing." He waved his hand in the direction of the hedge garden.

She lost her vision for a moment as her emotions soared out her ears. "Sensitive? Is that what I am?" She turned to the man at her side. "Did you hear that? Sensitive?"

Mr. Lawrence cleared his throat. "I think I might step out. Are you all right here?" Mr. Lawrence looked toward her, but she hardly saw. "Yes, yes, go if you must."

"Very good." Mr. Lawrence slipped out. "I'll be within calling distance if assistance is required."

Oscar watched through the crack, presumably to see Mr. Lawrence walk away. "And were you enjoying yourself?"

"Pardon?" His tone and question took her off guard.

"Here alone in the stables?" He pointed toward the crack in the door. "With Mr. Lawrence?"

"Of all the ridiculous... coming from you."

"Coming from me? I suppose you're referring to Miss Penny."

"To whom else would I be referring?" Eva placed both hands firmly on her hips again, rocking back and forth from heel to toe.

"You are changing the subject."

"I'm not. You are, certainly. For aren't we meant to be

talking about why you are kissing and flirting with me, and then found alone with Miss Penny, accepting her advances, making an utter rake of yourself?" She breathed out, stunned at her own bravery.

"A rake! You are calling me a rake now?"

"I—I am not." She breathed out. "But you are acting like one. Can you not simply walk in the gardens without entertaining a flirtation?"

He seemed to relax. But then tensed again. "And this Mr. Lawrence. What is he to you?"

"As I have inferred, you have no right to ask such things of me. Did you not suggest that I would do well to be warmer to others? To converse? To entertain men? To mend my *cold* reputation."

He grimaced. "I did. Of course. But hiding in a barn to be alone is not what I had in mind."

"You suggest we were behaving in an untoward manner?" She stepped nearer.

"No, of course not, but I—I do not like thinking of it." The defeat in his face touched her, but not enough.

"Oh, don't you? And do you think I like seeing you with Miss Penny? Just the sight brings back so much that is unpleasant." She looked away, barely able to swallow. "It's not just you. But everything."

"I could only imagine what you might be thinking as you have not said as much to me. I can see that I have errantly, unknowingly, caused you great pain. As that is the furthest design in my mind, might I explain, please?" The pleading in his face touched her and she huffed out a minor resignation.

She opened her mouth but then closed it again. "Certainly."

"I went to the hedge gardens to be alone. She came

upon me while I was entertaining the young Oscar and quite literally threw herself at me right at the moment that you came around the corner."

Eva could hardly believe her ears. "And I'm supposed to believe that coincidentally I saw you at just the right moment to witness an accidental embrace?"

"Yes, of course. If I say it is so."

She pressed her lips together. She wanted to believe him. And that was the problem. He seemed utterly without any guile. She wished so much that he was true. But what kind of woman fell for the same guise twice? She'd always assumed Lord Thomason to be quite in love with her. Every explanation for the friendliness with ladies had always been received as truth to her. Then to find out… "That's the crux of it, isn't it? All I know is what you tell me."

"And shouldn't that be enough? Come, Eva. I won't have you disbelieve my words, my honest pledge."

"Your… pledge?" She sucked in her breath.

"You won't hear me. And I'm only half ready to say such things, but I must. I cannot think of you entertaining others, without first knowing how I feel. Please, might I express myself?"

"I don't know if you should…" A great fear mixed with hope plagued her with confusion. If he loved her, she was afraid of what might happen next. If he didn't love her, she couldn't bear it.

"I must. Please hear me out." He reached for her hands and held them in his own. "I cannot be silent. I've asked for your patience, but you must know. I have learned from your uncle and made some investments. Things are lining up for me to be quite prepared to… to marry."

She felt her own mouth drop, but closed it directly.

He stepped closer and rested a hand at the side of her face. "My dear Eva."

She lifted her lashes and couldn't help but lean into his hand. Oh, she loved this man. The realization shocked her. And she could not speak for many moments.

"Eva, I do this all for you. I've been able to think of nothing else. You have become my future. The only one I can even remotely imagine. Will you… can you…"

Her heart hammered inside. Was she happy? Afraid? She was most certainly afraid. She almost leapt away in a panic thinking he meant to propose.

"Will you wait for me so that I might court you properly?"

Her shoulders relaxed. So much relief flowed through her, but she couldn't be at ease. Her palms were damp, her head felt chilled and her breath came short. "I'm sorry. I must go ask for some tea or something."

"Come. I will escort you there."

"Thank you." Her knees went weak. She felt wobbly on her feet and was grateful for Mr. Easton's arm to lean upon.

"Might I hope that you have an answer for me? That this bout of dizziness is not a negative but a positive reaction?"

Her mouth went dry, and she had no words. But she indicated they walk toward the house.

When close enough, they made it through a servants' door and straight to the kitchen.

She sat at a table while Mr. Easton asked one of Cook's assistants for a cup of tea. She was nearly in a panic. He would expect an answer, and she couldn't. She daren't give him one. Mr. Thomason's face flashed before her eyes—his smile, his promises, his lies, his flirting and the ladies, their derision, everyone in the room knowing how utterly foolish she was. She shook her head. "No."

"No?" He leaned forward. "Surely you do not mean…"

"No. I cannot. Mr. Easton. Please do not pursue this course. It will lead to nothing but hurt and sorrow for us both."

"How can you say that? How can you deny the happiness that I know you have when we are together?"

"By telling you quite plainly that I feel nothing of it now. Only dread and worry and a great panic." She tried to offer some sort of conciliation, but her hands shook and her mouth lowered and she could find nothing more to say.

"That is your answer."

"Yes. I'm… I'm sorry."

He waited, staring into her face for about ten very ragged breaths and then stood. "This is all you wish to say?"

"This is all."

"Very well then." He turned and walked out of the kitchen.

Part of her wanted to run after him. But the stronger, panicked side instead ran for her rooms.

She burst through her door. "Remy!"

"Yes, my lady."

"We must go. Now!"

"I'm almost finished packing."

"Oh, bless you." She collapsed onto her bed, tears welling up inside. Did she love Mr. Easton? Blast her traitorous heart. She loved him. Which made everything twice as difficult. She had been unwise to come to the house party in the first place and doubly unwise to invite someone as reasonable and easy to know as Mr. Easton. Of course her lonely heart would love him. She had never counted on him pursuing her. She just couldn't fathom why he would, how he had determined her to be the love of his life.

Just then, the loud voices of women's chatter walked past her door.

"Of course he would pursue her, ugly as she is. Have you heard what her dowry is?" Miss Penny sounded as smug as ever. "Naturally he enjoys my company, told me himself that I'm lovelier, but I can't help things if it's coming down to money, can I? My dowry is of course respectable…" The voices faded away.

She was powerless before her worst memory. Lord Thomason embracing another, murmuring sweetness in her ears. "Love her? No. I only love you. Who could love a woman with a face like hers? When I have such loveliness before me?"

Eva's hands shook. Everything felt the same as her first engagement. It all felt just like last time. Only worse, so much worse. For now, she knew the depths of love, and those depths led to a hurt like she'd never known.

Chapter Eighteen

Oscar watched the others start placing greenery. He leaned on a doorframe, wanting to do his duty to his host, but not having the energy to actually enter the room. It had been one hour since Eva had turned him down, looking as though she were breaking her own heart as well as his. And he just didn't have it in him to participate in much.

Suddenly home was the place he most wanted to be. He could involve his brothers in his new shipping venture. He could play with Tabitha's lads, and enjoy Cook's meals. If she would not have him, why was he even here? Mind made up, he turned and stumbled when a soft body entered his arms.

He tried to step back to steady this person, when lips met his. But not Eva's lips. He grabbed her shoulders and held back a giggling Miss Penny. She placed a hand at her mouth. "I didn't think I dared." She giggled again, looking around at who might have seen them.

"What has come over you?" He wiped his mouth with the back of his hand.

She pointed up.

Mistletoe.

"Confound it."

A swift glance around the room showed many amused guests, but not Lady Evaline. Thank heavens for that. Then movement distracted him. Out in the great hall, a brightly colored dress came into view. Eva wiped her eyes and hurried past.

Without another look at Miss Penny's blushing face, he ran after Eva.

Quickly she had moved outside and was climbing into her carriage.

"What's this?"

She turned away. Her footman shut the door.

He opened the carriage door and sat beside her. "You're leaving?"

"Yes." She sniffed. Her red eyes frustrated him even more.

"You're miserable."

She nodded.

"Then why are you leaving? It's not what you think."

"I wish that were true. But I've been in this situation before. I'm not doing this again. Please exit the carriage."

"Eva, please you have to believe me. Stay."

She lifted her chin. A new fire was in her eyes. "No. I don't *have* to do anything. That's what you don't understand. I don't need you. You might need me and my dowry, but I have no need of you. Now, if you don't leave my carriage, I will ask my footman to show you out."

He searched her face. "You would throw me out?"

"You would flirt with and kiss another?"

He opened his mouth and then closed it. Then opened it again. "I told you that is not what it seems."

"And I told you I've been here before. Goodbye, Mr. Easton."

He stepped out of the carriage, not knowing what else to do. He'd told her Miss Penny was nothing to him. How did one prove such a thing? If she didn't believe him, he had nothing else to say.

As her carriage drove away, he realized she'd never as yet used his first name.

He turned back to the house and almost bumped into Mr. Shaw. "Oh, excuse me, sir."

"I think you and I should have a conversation."

"Certainly." He followed him in through the front door where more people than he would like were gathered to witness his and Eva's business. Mr. Talmus laughed with his friends. "Lady Snow." He shook his head and the others raised pretend glasses in his direction.

"Don't listen to them." Mr. Shaw led him to his study, told him to sit and handed him a glass of brandy. "Lady Evaline is a special woman."

"Yes, she said you were close."

"Special to me, yes, but special in general. She has a beautiful heart and wants nothing more than to help others and to connect with people."

He snorted. "You know they call her Lady Snow. I'm beginning to understand why. I regret I didn't heed their warnings."

"Tosh. You are hearing the pride of spurned men. And nothing more. She was hurt, gravely so. And everyone in the ton seemed to be in on the joke. Everywhere she turned, the women were talking about the most wanted lord who promised to still be available to them all—after all he was only marrying the venerable and so called ugly, Lady Evaline for her dowry."

"Ugly? How could she be ugly?" Oscar was shaken. "I knew it was hard on her, but… was she on betting books and talked of then for her looks?"

"Yes. Imagine the worst. And then when she spurned him? They all felt spurned, like she ruined their joke."

Oscar shook his head. "No wonder she acts like she'd like to disappear and never see anyone again."

"She would. She only came because I asked particularly that she would."

"Hm."

"And when she invited you, thinking her heart was safe, I thought there was a chance, that you two might find a way…" He watched Oscar and something about his hopeful expression sat wrong.

"I sympathize. More than that. I do feel for her." Oscar clasped his hands together in a moment of nervous energy. "But there are two people involved here, and I've just been on the receiving end of her cold rejection. I'm going to need some time." He had to get his life in order and his finances ready anyway.

"You won't go after her?"

He shook his head before words could come. "I've just been almost forcibly thrown from her carriage. I don't think she would take too kindly to me right now." And he was not going anywhere near her only to be soundly rejected again.

"I suppose you're correct."

"In fact, perhaps you won't mind if I take my leave as well?"

"Oh, certainly."

"My family is together, and I'd like to run some of these investment ideas by them… and I miss them."

Mr. Shaw stood. "I'm pleased you could come. And I wish you every happiness."

Oscar eyed him with suspicion. "Your well wishes are not necessary."

His host leaned his head back and laughed. "Oh, you're as stubborn as she is."

"And now that we've established her great stubbornness, you must know that a man can only ask so many times and be soundly rejected before he moves on." There he'd said it. He held out his hand. "Thank you for your kindness. I'll be on my way."

"You're most welcome."

Oscar wished to wipe the overly pleased expression off of Mr. Shaw's face. What that man thought he knew, Oscar could never guess.

When Oscar entered his room, Reed was already packing.

"Very good."

"Thank you, my lord."

"We go home."

He nodded.

"I'd like to leave within the hour."

"We'll be ready."

Oscar didn't want to stand around watching his valet, nor did he wish to be openly gawked at and discussed by other members of the party. He gathered his correspondence and took out paper and quill and decided he may as well focus on his new industry, the new purpose to his life.

An hour later, with seven more letters in hand to various possible investors, as well as a renowned captain, Oscar followed his trunks down the stairs and climbed into his carriage.

The ground was still covered in snow, but just as Eva

had done, he'd stubbornly insisted on leaving and asked that sledging blades be attached to his equipage. The snow had taken a break from falling and the sun was out, but everyone was talking about how they were thinking it would start up again in a couple days. Somebody's elbow was acting up again. And because he'd so accurately predicted the first fall, everyone was inclined to believe him. The sledding blades allowed him to pull ahead of most carriages. His own horses comfortable in the snow, he knew he would arrive home much faster than any in such a long string of carriages. He could only hope that Lady Evaline would find her way. She was in good hands. He refused to continue chasing the woman. He would give her some time, arrange his own affairs and then reach out. Perhaps later she'd feel more warmly toward him.

As he pulled out onto the main thoroughfare, they exchanged the blades for wheels again. The roads were clear of snow but undeniably muddy. He settled back against his seat with a book in hand, hoping not to be tortured by thoughts of Eva the entire journey.

Chapter Nineteen

Eva fidgeted in her seat. Mrs. Widget had fallen asleep hours past. She'd not seen a hair of her the entire party, but she seemed ready to leave at a moment's notice. Eva smiled, thinking of her memory of Mr. Shaw. She was a dear woman. And now, considering her in a new light, Eva had a new understanding of her loneliness, of the life she lead. Would that be Eva's life? The entirety of her life? No family, no siblings, no friends? No marriage?

Eva had a three days' journey ahead of her. The snow had abated. And she'd told the coachman to push the horses while the roads were clear of snow, but the going was slow. Melted snow meant mud.

Her mind kept replaying all her interactions with Mr. Easton. Their shared kiss burned her lips whenever her thoughts lingered on that memory. His eyes, always so kind. His jealousy. She tapped her fan in her lap. What disturbed her most right now? No matter what he said, she kept seeing him with other women, enjoying their attentions.

She'd been in this situation before. She wanted to trust him. She pulled off her gloves in frustration. Why had he not followed her? Would that not be one more proof of his caring? But would she have received him? She sighed. Probably not. How could she know? How could she trust?

Their carriage slowed to a stop. "What's this?"

Her coachman's face appeared in the opening above her head. "We're turning north at the divide. Looks like everyone is travelling today." The cross section of roads where everyone went either on the north road toward Scotland or south toward London. She was going north, and she knew whenever Mr. Easton left the party, he would be going south. This divide felt like much more.

"How long will we be waiting?"

"Hard to tell, my lady. We have a good line of carriages in front. Looks as though there's a bit of trouble with some mud."

"Thank you."

He closed the hatch. And Eva sat back in a huff. Her aunt slept on. Remy was perpetually devoid of conversation. Eva thought she might die of anxious boredom. Was that possible? To be anxiously bored? It seemed as though it were, because she could no longer bear her carriage and its dull worry. She opened the door and wished to step out, to walk beside her equipage, but the deep ruts, the mud on both sides, the line of carriages and hacks and working carts both to the front and behind her, discouraged her. So, she closed the door and opened the window instead, sticking her head out as far as it would go.

The air was delightfully crisp. And fresh. As they drew closer to the road where she would turn permanently away from Mr. Easton, she wondered when he would pass this way. In a few days? After Christmas? What would her father say when she arrived home Christmas day? Dear Mr. Shaw. Hopefully he understood her abrupt departure.

Misgivings became the queen of her emotions. Had she reacted too strongly to Mr. Easton? Was it so very bad for him to show an interest in her? To receive attention from other ladies? She cringed. It was so very bad for her. She couldn't go through another situation like the one she had.

Clouds had started to gather overhead, the low-lying dark grey that meant snow. Were they to have worse weather? Their carriage inched forward. Noise up ahead drew her attention. It looked as though servants were working to free carriages. This might be a very long wait indeed.

Her coachman opened the hatch. "It might be several hours yet. And it looks like snow."

"Thank you. We're a bit trapped here, aren't we?"

"That we are, my lady. Are you warm enough?"

"Yes, thank you. Have you hot bricks with you as well?"

"Aye, we have. Thank you. If anything changes, I'll let you know." He shut the hatch again.

She had three days of travel north, but only one south. If the weather started to get really bad, perhaps she could make her way south? Why did she want to go south? Who would she see in the south? The Eastons. Mr. Easton. He would travel south eventually.

And she was going to follow him? Just drive after him in her carriage? To where he would eventually travel? Did she know where the Easton's lived?

Reluctantly, she admitted that she did. The snow started to fall in earnest. "This doesn't look good." She closed her window.

They creeped forward though, so perhaps she could get

on her way before she was completely trapped in the middle of the road.

But on they waited. She dozed for a bit and when she awoke, the snow was still falling and the ground everywhere was covered in white.

She tapped on the roof.

The coachman appeared in the small opening and his kindly face comforted her. But he shook his head. "We've had a bit of bad news, confirmed a moment ago."

"Bad news?"

"Yes. The road to the north is completely blocked."

She gasped.

"There's been a carriage accident. There's a long line after it, and with all the snow none of them are able to turn about and return and if they did, they couldn't get through this complete block either."

"Oh dear. What can we do?"

"There's no turning back to Mr. Shaw's, at least not yet. I can see carriages waiting for miles behind us, I can."

"And to the south?" Curse her wretched half-hope when she knew she had just denied the man any kind of hope for himself.

"That's our best chance. I'm wondering if there might be an inn with a room."

"Excellent thoughts. I have friends we can stay with as well." She swallowed. Did the Eastons count as friends? What was she doing, precisely? It was all instinct. She was in need, alone on the road with an old, sleeping aunt and servants. Mr. Easton would help. His family would as well. They seemed like the decent sort of people left in the world. Yet, maybe they would try an inn first.

Another hour passed and they were at last able to make

the turn to the south. The road was full of carriages but at least they were moving. However slowly.

It was long past light before they pulled into the first inn. Signs everywhere announced no vacancy. They rested a moment, refreshed themselves. Carriages passed by them still heading South.

"Oh dear."

Their coachman kept on. Later into the night they travelled.

Her aunt at last awoke. "Goodness child, what are you about?"

"Oh, Auntie. We are driving through the night trying to find an inn to rest in. The road north is closed."

"Good heavens."

"Don't worry, the coachman knows what he's about."

She nodded and fidgeted for a moment. But after looking out into the darkness and then adjusting her seat, she nodded. "And he's got it all managed?"

"Yes, we are in good hands."

"Very well then." She leaned her head back and closed her eyes again.

Eva shook her head. That woman could sleep through anything. She was the perfect companion, just as Mr. Easton had said. The pang in her heart sharpened. She missed him. Was it so wrong to encourage a relationship of sorts? Could she not court him? Get to know him?

The sigh that left her body carried with it such a weight. The longer they rode along on this lonely road into a scary unknown, the longer she considered her plight if she chose to be alone the rest of her days. Relying only on servants or distant relatives for company.

They travelled another couple of hours. The road became less crowded, but the inns were still full. At last in the early light of morning, they arrived at one that at least didn't have no vacancy signs posted. As the coachman ran in through deep, thick snow, she held her breath. He was there a bit longer than the others, and she hoped against hope that at last she would have a comfortable place to rest her head. The snow was thick. They wouldn't be travelling at all for much longer if they couldn't find a place to rest. He came back out and instead of climbing up on top again, waited at her window.

"Do you have news?"

"They don't have room, but I asked about nearby estates and they said there's a family up the road there who are the best in the area, kinder than any, and that they might provide some shelter at least."

"Where are we? Which county?"

"Westchester."

Her voice cracked when she said, "What is the family name?"

"Easton, my lady."

Her hand went to her heart without thinking. "How far down the road?"

"It will take some time, perhaps another hour or more, but I think we will have better luck trying this than if we keep on going down this road." His face was lined, his eyes tired. And she knew the horses were needing to stop as well. "Thank you. Let's go to the Easton's', then, shall we?"

A lump grew in her throat. How could she possibly arrive at their home in such a state? What would Mr. Easton think of her when he saw her in his home? Would he even want to speak to her? Probably not, but at least she knew they wouldn't turn her away.

They started on their way but didn't go much further

JEN GEIGLE JOHNSON

before the whole carriage wobbled and then one side tipped precariously to the earth. "Oh dear."

Her aunt awoke. "Oh my, oh dear. What is happening?"

"I think we've lost a wheel."

"Where are we? Heavens, child! Are we lost? Are we alone?" She held one hand to her mobcap and the other to her heart.

"Not at all."

The coachman came round to her door again. "We've lost the wheel. What say you about me sending Jacques to the Eastons' home and enquiring after some help?"

She nodded. "I see no other option. And, Henry. You may sit inside with us, please do, while we wait."

"Thank you, my lady. I will manage the horses and then I'd like that very much." He clapped his hands together and she understood that his fingers must be cold even under his thick gloves.

Watching the footman ride out into the night toward the family of the one person she trusted to help her right now was in some ways comforting and in others, terrifying. If she turned to him, would he stay? Or would he be enticed away by the nearest pretty face? She replaced her gloves. Patted down her skirts. She knew she must look a sight, travelling all night long, but it couldn't be helped. Nothing could be helped. She sat up as tall as she could... and waited.

Chapter Twenty

❦

Oscar was astounded at the loud banging on the front door. He hurried down the stairs. He had just arrived and still wore his travelling clothes. Their butler, Hansen, answered the door with Oscar right behind him.

"Begging your pardon, sir, we had a carriage accident up the road there and I have a lady with her aunt who have nowhere to stay tonight. Might they come here?"

"Of course. Down the road, you say?"

"Yes, in that direction, just around the bend from the inn."

"I'll go immediately."

"Yourself, Mr. Easton?" His Butler looked as though he would complain.

"I'm dressed. It might as well be me as anyone. Who is the lady?"

"Lady Evaline. We come from far north, by way of a house party. The northern roads were all closed. We've been looking for an inn all night without any luck."

His heart might have forgotten to function as he held his breath. Oscar battled wonder, anger, hope, and despair in a matter of moments. How was one to act? "I'll be going." His whole body responded with a great protective urgency. "But perhaps we need to consider carefully. Are the roads passable by carriage?"

"At first, yes. But we lost a wheel. They were getting bad, worse while I've been travelling here."

He nodded, quickly formulating a plan. "I'll go on horseback. We need three of our stable hands as well, the aunt might find it disruptive, but it cannot be helped. You have a coachman? Who else?" He knew, or he'd remembered, that she had no one else.

"That is all. Lady Evaline, and her aunt, maid, and coachman."

Oscar tore out to the stables but called over his shoulder. "Prepare rooms."

"Very good, Mr. Easton, sir."

He saddled his own horse, then he rested a hand against her flank. "Easy girl. We have a special person to bring back to the house." How had this come to be? Tabitha's lads would surely blame Father Christmas. He leapt up on his horse and rode out into the snow. The road had melted and then frozen and then covered in snow. But as he picked his way in the frozen brush on the side, through deep snow, he found the horse could manage. Eventually he heard others behind him, and their rescue party moved as quickly as they could, which unfortunately was still an agonizing pace.

Snow fell all around him, making visibility difficult, but at last up ahead, a carriage, tilted precariously to the side and covered in a new layer of snow, sat like a beacon. "Eva!" His voice felt lost to the quiet snow, muffled, but she popped her head out. He couldn't stop the grin that filled his face. "Eva!"

"Mr. Easton?" She fumbled with the door. "Is that you?"

"Yes! It's me! You're but a mile from my house."

She made to step out into the snow but then wobbled on her feet. "It's deep."

"Yes. Wait there." He rode close, until he was at her side. She looked more beautiful than ever to his tired eyes. Then he peered in. "Footmen are here to take Mrs. Widget, your good man, and maid back to the house with us. I'm afraid we're all going horseback, and slowly at that. Are you all prepared?"

"The trunks?"

"The footmen will take care of them. And unfortunately, we will have to come back for your carriage when the snow melts."

She nodded.

"Unless you need to be on your way much sooner?" He searched her face.

"I have nowhere else to go." Her eyes widened, and he almost saw the bit of a quiver on her lips. His arm swept down, reached for her arm and shoulder and pulled her up onto the front of his horse. "There's nowhere else I'd want you to be." He wrapped his arms around her, turned his horse and headed back to the Easton estate. "You know, my family is going to love you."

"I am sorry to interrupt your family celebrations."

"As far as I'm concerned, they aren't family celebrations unless you're there." He nuzzled her neck. "I don't know how, or why, but I refuse to believe your coming is up to chance. This is your new family, if you'll let it be. Please allow me to court you. I am sincere."

The pause was thick but not uncomfortable. Then her nod, brief though it was, sent such a happiness through him he was immediately warmed through. "The lads are going to love you. I call them the lads. No one can tell them apart. Not even Henry. Of course their mother can. Tabitha Cat. That's what I call my sister Tabitha, and I will tell you she much prefers Tabitha. Which is precisely why we all still call her Tabitha Cat. She is the easiest of the bunch and if you hear Edward going off about how he beats me at… anything, don't listen to half what he says, because that's about how often he really does win at anything." Oscar sighed. "Edward is a good man. He's doing his best by all of us." His embrace tightened around her, pulling her closer. "I know I've said all that before." He laughed at himself. "I'm happy you're here. At last my Christmas feels complete."

"I'm sorry I misjudged you."

He shook his head. "No apologies. You did everything just right. How else were you supposed to behave, what else were you supposed to think? My task? To spend the rest of my days proving my love and loyalty to you." As the words left his lips, he knew they were true. He knew, more than anything, he wanted to marry this woman.

She didn't answer, but leaned back against him in such a comfortable and trusting manner that he cradled her ever closer. He sat up taller, realizing anew the precious cargo he held.

THE MORNING BROKE EARLY, AND OSCAR WAS UP WITH THE sun. Today was a day for celebrations. And he couldn't wait to see the faces of all his family when they met Eva. He grinned. He was up and dressed way earlier than usual.

Noises came from the nursery down the hall, which was connected to Tabitha and Henry's bedroom. The boys were up, and their nursemaid was attempting to quiet the ruckus but to no avail.

"But we want to go outside now. If we wait for later, people will have already walked in it."

"Tosh, child. Who is going to be out walking in the snow at this hour. Now come. Let's get started on our studies and get them finished so that when others do awake, you'll be free to play."

"Studies! It's Christmas Eve."

Oscar stepped into the room.

"Uncle Oscar!" The boys jumped up and ran to him, leaping up into his arms.

"Did I hear someone say it's Christmas Eve?"

"Yes! It is!"

"No, it couldn't be."

"It is, I tell you. And we wish to go outside."

He glanced at the nurse who seemed more relieved than anything that he had arrived. "I could use some strong helpers this morning."

The eldest stood taller. "We are the ones for the job."

"Excellent. Get your warm gear on. We are going outside."

Their cheers were loud enough to wake the whole family wing, and Oscar laughed even louder. "This home needs more boughs of green. I say we go a hunting for holly."

"I can do that!"

"And we need another tree," Oscar added with a wink. "I'll bring the ax."

Their jumping and cheering made him laugh all the more. Soon Tabitha stood in the doorway, Henry right behind. "Oscar?" Tabitha's confused happiness made him grin. "Sister. I'm borrowing your boys as they're the most capable helpers around. And everyone else is lazing about the day."

"Did we hear someone arrive last night?"

His grin only grew. "Yes."

The couple shared a look and then back at him. "And?"

"She's probably still sleeping at this unholy hour."

"She? And?" Tabitha's eyes were shining, and Oscar could only be happy he was bringing more happiness to her life.

"And, I can't make any promises. She's got opinions of her own of course, but I'm working on getting you another sister..."

She squealed and ran to him, throwing her arms around his neck. "Shall I put up some mistletoe?"

Henry groaned.

"Oh stop, you should be happiest of all at the prospect of some mistletoe."

"Too true. Could you hang some right... here?" He held a hand up above his head.

She laughed and embraced her husband. Oscar turned to the boys. "Be ready to go down by the front door in five minutes."

"Yes, sir." They ran to their nurse, begging to get ready for the day.

When Oscar was dressed for the out of doors, he made his way downstairs and found Edward sitting in his office as though he'd been there for hours. His hair was ruffled and his face looked drawn.

"Brother."

His head lifted and the smile that filled his face pinged Oscar's previously angry heart.

"I heard tell that a mangy brother of mine had made his way back for Christmas."

"That I have, with a guest."

Edward's eyebrows rose.

"Now, I haven't convinced her yet. I'm counting on the rest of you to prove that being a Easton is the best thing she could imagine, even if she has to put up with me."

Edward approached and held out his hand. "I'm happy for you, brother. She couldn't have found a better man."

They embraced and Oscar at last felt things return to what they once were between them. "I have things to tell you, brother. I've learned how to make a living."

"What was this house party you went to?"

"It's good news for the lot of us I believe. Opportunities for all."

"I look forward to hearing it." The hope in Edward's eyes made Oscar smile despite their earlier conversations.

Oscar clapped his brother on the shoulder. "You bear too much of this on your own. Come, close this door. Enjoy your family. All will be well."

Edward's face pinched with worry and then he nodded. "Too true. There's nothing in here that can't wait until after Twelfth Night."

"That's the spirit! Now the lads and I are heading outside to get us some greenery and another tree. We might build a fort and a snowman while we're out there. You are welcome to join us."

He straightened and rotated his shoulders. "You'll never get a tree chopped down without me."

"Oh, I don't know about that, but we could try our hand at it again, couldn't we?"

"We absolutely should."

Oscar stood by the front door waiting for his helpers to join him when Eva arrived at the top of the stairs.

Her hair was tied in a single braid at her neck. She stood tall, but her shoulders were relaxed. Her dress looked comfortable, a soft velvet that flowed to her toes. He wanted to wrap his arms around her and feel the soft fabric in his hands. "Eva."

Her smile grew. She stepped down the stairs and something about seeing her in his home, with his family, on the stairs he'd climbed from when he himself was a lad burned his stomach around in happy ways. "Fancy seeing you here." He stepped to her, yet his feet couldn't get there fast enough. As they met on a middle stair, she was at once in his arms just as he'd wished.

"You're here." He pulled her as close as she would fit against him.

She nodded into him.

"I hope you'll stay?"

She nodded again.

He wanted to say, forever, but he bit the word before it slipped. She was not ready, not yet, and he had yet to hear back from the ship builders.

"I'm going to find and cut a tree."

She stepped away. "Are you?"

"Yes, Edward and the lads and I are going to bring back some greenery and another tree, then we'll meet for breakfast. But if you walk down that hallway there... in fact, come with me." His grin grew. She laughed and took his hand as they hurried to the kitchen.

The closer they came, the better the smells, the warmer the air, and the friendlier the chatter until he stepped into the bright kitchen. Mrs. Channing had everyone busy with the midday meal. Trays were already prepared for break-fast. He watched for a moment. "That's our cook."

Eva nodded, watching him more than the kitchen which he didn't mind one bit. When he cleared his throat, Mrs. Channing dropped everything and came. "You're returned, Mr. Easton. It's good to see you." She bobbed a curtsey to him and waited expectantly.

"Mrs. Channing. This is Lady Evaline."

Eva surprised them both and reached out for a hug. "I've heard wonderful things about you. I'm so happy to meet you."

Their embrace tightened everything in Oscar's chest in a happy sort of painful joy. "I wonder if you could look after this lady here while I go out and terrorize the forest?"

"I would love nothing more. Master Oscar has brought you to the right place. You'll forgive me, when I see his face, I can't think of him as anything but a lad."

"Perhaps you have some stories to share?" Eva's wicked smile made Oscar laugh.

"Not too many, I expect."

"Oh, I have stories for you, don't you worry about that. Now you sit right here, and I'll get something warm inside you."

"She was up all night in a carriage in the snowstorm."

That had the whole room clucking over Eva. He left her in their capable hands.

Feeling like a stuffed rooster filled with satisfaction, he ran to the front door where the lads were nearly bursting outside without him. Edward arrived and then Henry as well. Edward clapped him on the shoulder in a tight embrace. "Good to have you home, brother."

It was good to be home.

Chapter Twenty-One

✦✦✦

After a more than filling breakfast in the kitchen, Eva sat again with the family for another meal with everyone now awake and returned in their dining room. If she hadn't loved Oscar before spending time with Mrs. Channing, she certainly loved him now. Three more Easton brothers, Edward, Julian, and Tauncy sat with her. Watching their similar laughs and their similar mouths, she could only sit back in wonder at this singular family of good men.

They were finishing up their meal when Edward sat back in his chair. "Tell us, Lady Evaline, how did you meet my brother?"

She smiled to herself and then looked to Oscar for guidance.

"I asked her to dance and she turned me down at Almack's."

"No!" Tabitha looked about as horrified as Eva probably should have felt. She cringed still at the thought.

Then she shook her head. "But that was not the first time I met him."

"Ah, so you remember." Oscar's pleased face gave her more courage.

"I do. I was at my very first ball of my very first Season. And I had lost a slipper."

His eyes shone, laughter brimming up in them.

"And your good brother retrieved it, amidst the line of dancers, and brought it to me." She smiled at the memory.

"Too true. That little shoe was being kicked about by every Hessian in the place. I took my life in my hands going after it. I missed a boot in the face from the Duke of Grenville and received a none too pleased glare from his wife."

They laughed together, the warmth in the room filling more of her lonely places, holding her close in a family sized embrace. "Did you really turn him down when he asked you dance?" Tabitha's concerned face brought a new appreciation for a sibling in one's life.

"I did. But it was a great misunderstanding. I would never do such a thing again." She considered telling the story of her falling turban when Oscar stood. "I have something for you."

He left and for a moment or two, everyone waited in silence. Then Edward shook his head. "He better not be going to find his old toy soldiers."

Everyone laughed until he hurried back in. When Eva saw the black fabric in his hands, her eyes filled with tears. "Oh."

"I have been meaning to return this." He handed back a carefully folded arm band she had worn to remember her mother's mourning. "It seems I am to be forever retrieving errant articles of clothing for our Lady Evaline."

She reached for the bit of fabric, holding it close. "Yes, this was headed for a dousing in lemonade."

Eva was astounded he still had it, and suddenly, her mother felt closer than ever. She turned to the group who waited patiently, confusion on their faces. She reverently unfolded the arm band. It still had the pin attached. Her smile grew. "My mother passed away and I was recently out of mourning, wearing this arm band. It means more to me now, to have thoughts of her be part of such a meaningful time in my life here with all of you." She said no more for a moment, but in her heart she hoped that somehow, somewhere her mother was looking down on them all. "I flung my arm out in the dance and it sailed off my wrist, out over the tops of all the dancers, right for the lemonade."

They gasped. "And I rescued it." Oscar puffed out his chest.

"That's quite a story." Edward looked from one to the other of them, shaking his head.

Their conversation was meaningful, pleasant, some of the most enjoyable that Eva had ever experienced. And then one by one, they stood.

"Shall we take a walk about the grounds?" Tabitha smiled. Then she clung to her for most of the afternoon. As they laughed together, Eva recognized the friend she had not yet ever had. Her heart started to relax, the trust she wanted to feel started to grow, and she began to fall in love with the Easton family.

She saw Oscar now and again throughout the day. He checked in on her regularly but seemed busy with his family. Soon after he arrived, the home had doubled its greenery, another tree was up and decorations out. Talk of mistletoe and the yule log were everywhere.

Even though she was sleepy from her journey, she didn't

want to miss anything by sleeping away the afternoon, so she found her way into the library. Their impressive collection made her love the family all the more. As she walked down a long wall filled with floor to ceiling with books, she knew hours of enjoyment were ahead of her.

"So this is where you have found yourself." Oscar's smile was so much warmer and more natural here at home. There was an added wholesome look to his normal rugged handsomeness, and she was drawn to him more than ever.

"What an amazing collection."

"Yes, both of my parents loved to read. They took great pride in these books. They read every single one."

"That's incredible."

"Hmm. I agree. I've read quite a few myself. It has been my goal to finish them all."

"Then I shall join you."

He stopped closer and reached for her hand. "That could take a long time."

She nodded.

"A very long time." He watched her.

"I hope it does." Her hope bubbled up, powerfully, giving her courage.

"Perhaps even a lifetime?" His eyes held a hint of insecurity but mostly answered hope... and love. He led her over by the fire. "Now, shall we talk about how you are here in the first place? I haven't heard the story of my most favorite Christmas gift."

She laughed. And felt her cheeks heat. But she shrugged. "We were travelling home, but after a very long, hours long, wait to turn onto the north road, we turned and then we heard that it was blocked. Apparently several carriage accidents caused quite a lineup. So with snow starting to fall fast, we turned south. Every inn on the way was full. The last inn suggested a nice family down the road…" As she looked into his face, she wanted to be as honest as possible. "But I admit to hoping to find you when we turned to go south. Were we to find an inn, once we awakened from whatever inn I hoped to find, my next stop was going to be here."

He pulled her into his arms, and she felt the familiar peace that came when Oscar was near. "You were coming to find me." His voice was full of wonder. He stared down into her face with such a look of love she thought he would kiss her. She thought for sure she would be lost to his embrace. But instead, he tucked her hair behind her ear. "I love you, Eva. I want you in my life forever. I know I have promises to make yet, but they're coming. Stay with us. Stay at least until Twelfth Night."

She nodded. "I'll stay. The snow wouldn't let me leave anyway. My carriage is broken. I'm trapped."

"Trapped, are you?" The mischief, the tease in his eyes made her laugh.

"Yes, trapped, by more than our circumstances. I love you too, Oscar. And that binds me to you more than anything else."

His smile tickled her insides. "Then we are standing in the perfect place." He looked up.

When she saw mistletoe directly above their heads, her grin grew. "You planned that!"

"Of course I did."

"Then what are you waiting for?"

His arms wrapped more fully around her, filling her with a sense of security that, once she'd finally tasted, she never wanted to live without. She knew he was her future. The lips that covered hers sealed her love and, in a way, her fate. She could no sooner resist this man than resist the taking in of her own breath. Her hands pulled him closer. She responded over and over again with an urgency that begged for more. Oscar dipped her low, holding her close.

And then cheering interrupted in the doorway.

All of the Easton's—Edward, Julian, Tauney, Tabitha, Henry and the lads—all cheered, their smiles large and full of love.

She pressed her hands to the sides of her face in embarrassment. But Tabitha shook her head. "No need for that. We're family."

Then Eva found herself embraced by each one, even the lads.

"And now it's time to light the yule log and read from Luke 2."

Oscar's hand captured hers as they made their way into the family's private sitting room. They gathered, each sitting in a favorite chair, the chairs occupied by their mother and father left empty and close to the fire. Eva caught a lump in her throat as Edward rested a strong hand on the back of one. Then he reached for a large, old and well-used Bible to read from the familiar chapter describing the world's first Christmas. She snuggled up in the crook of Oscar's arm as she listened.

"I noticed you used my name." His whisper made her laugh.

"Oscar."

"Mm. I love the sound of that."

"Oscar."

"Eva."

They whispered back and forth and the others smiled encouragingly on as Edward lit the Yule log and they each shared their favorite Christmas memories and thoughts of their parents. When it came to Oscar, he stood. "I have a new favorite Christmas memory, but I cannot tell you. I have to show you."

Everyone including Eva waited, curiosity growing.

"Tabitha, could you play the piano for us?"

Eva gasped. "Are you singing?"

The others guffawed with laughter and nodded when he shook his head. "*We* are."

They stared in amazement as she joined him. He handed music to Tabitha and the hymn they sang last in their caroling began at her fingertips.

"Just the last verse."

She nodded.

After a few strains, the rest of the Eastons took pity on him and joined them, singing the refrain and then song after song together, laughing and caroling. A new Easton tradition was born.

In the midst of it all, Oscar looked at Eva once more. "I love you. I do. This is the happiest Christmas I've ever spent here at home."

Eva knew it was the same for her and that she *was* home. Whatever came of their life together, whatever plans he had for his future, home would always be at his side.

Epilogue

Christmas came and went. The lads played with every toy and then played with them again. The family lazed about. And Eva fell more in love with them all every day.

At last Twelfth Night was upon them. She had said she would stay until Twelfth Night. But no plans had been mentioned of travel. No decisions made. She couldn't continue living forever at the Easton estate. Her Father had been notified. And he was pleased. Her Aunt seemed happy as ever. She'd taken residence in the library and Eva half suspected she herself would read the entire collection.

Oscar had been looking forward to the festivities probably more than anyone. Eva had watched in amazement as he planned with Cook and talked with great animation to Henry and Tabitha's boys. He'd coordinated all the games, and prepared a play and a poetry reading. They would have a musical performance, even a small dance. How did this family function without Oscar around?

Tabitha noticed her watching him finish tying some last

decorations on a mantle. She stepped up beside Eva. "This is all for you."

Eva's eyes widened.

"He's a great brother, don't misunderstand. And we love him dearly. But this Oscar, this is something altogether new. You bring out the best in him." Tabitha reached in for an embrace and surprised Eva with a kiss on her cheek.

"He's the best of men. I'm so happy here, with you, with him. I hope it never ends." Her wistful sigh did not go unnoticed, but she couldn't hide her great happiness, her hope to be together.

The family gathered for what looked to be a full evening. Eva had only heard the half of it which included Charades, readings, musical performances, and a duet by Eva and Oscar. She laughed when she thought of it. He was really committed to continuing their pattern of singing together.

The servants brought in a huge bowl. It sloshed around as they placed it on the table. Oscar clapped. "And now for some snap-dragon."

The lads ran to the table with Tabitha calling out, "Be careful."

"They'll be fine, Tabitha." Henry wrapped an arm across her shoulder. "Remember the fire doesn't burn."

She nodded, but Eva could tell it didn't sit well. She moved to stand beside one of the lads, and Tabitha smiled. "Thank you."

When they lit the brandy on fire and snuffed all the candles but one, the glow on the Eastons' faces made her laugh.

When it was her turn, she reached into the flames, amazed at the warmth that didn't burn her. She grabbed a fiery currant and popped it into her mouth, snuffing out the flames. The blue of the flames on her hand astonished her, and when she showed it to the lad at her side, his eyes widened. But she was ready when it was his turn. "See now, we don't touch our hair or our clothes. You ready to try?"

He nodded, but then didn't dare stick his hands through the fire.

Henry scooped him up. "I've got you. Let's do it together. And I'll eat the currant, because I guarantee you won't like it."

He nodded, and Eva smiled, watching father and son. Tabitha's eyes on the pair of them were full of adoration. And Eva knew she wanted that in her life.

Oscar watched her. When her gaze met his, he winked. She loved this man more than she ever thought she could love anyone. Everyone went around the bowl, taking turns eating the currants and playing the fire until they were all tired and ready for something else.

Once the snap-dragon was all cleaned up, the family gathered in a semicircle in their comfortable chairs around the fire. Edward stood and said lovely things about the East-on's year ahead about family goals, about their father. But she could only hear every other one of them. Oscar had taken her bare hand in his and his thumb, his fingers, his own skin on hers was sending fire up and down her arm. Every touch was a rush of tingles. Every movement a decla-ration of love.

At one point, Edward stopped talking and Oscar was on his knees in front of her.

"Oh!" Her eyes blurred with joy, and she leaned forward in her chair.

"Lady Evaline, my Eva, will you allow me to honor and cherish and love only you for the rest of our lives?"

She opened her mouth to answer, but Oscar held up a finger.

Edward cleared his throat. "You missed a part."

"I'm getting there, brother. Thank you."

"Oh, good show. Carry on."

"Will you let me awake early to stir the fire in the grate, order your tray for our breakfast in bed, buy you all manner of frivolous and brightly colored dresses and… take you on a voyage on my new ship?"

"What?"

He held up a finger again, and she laughed. "And. Will you please, make me more happy than I can imagine, and you as well, and do me the honor of being my wife, Mrs. Oscar Easton?"

She waited. "Are you finished?"

"Yes, that's all."

"Then yes, I will, to all of it. I would only be happy with you. And the rest of you. I am highly honored to become an Easton."

"It is a rather elevated name, nothing like being a lady or anything." Edward grinned.

The others laughed.

Oscar pulled her to her feet and kissed her soundly, until the lads started making sounds and complaining. "Thank you." He murmured against her lips.

"Hmm." She smiled.

Then Oscar and Eva turned to the family. Oscar held up their hands, tightly locked together. "Might I introduce my fiancée?"

Once all the embracing and the loving and the welcoming was finished, and they were once again seated, Eva squeezed his hand. "Can we talk about the new ship?"

She sat back, watching Oscar and his brothers excitedly

discuss their new venture in shipping. It seems half of the ton had heard and wanted to be a part, including her dear Uncle Shaw. She smiled ever broader as she considered her own wedding gift to Oscar. She'd spoken with her solicitor and by tomorrow, a new investor will have entered the Easton shipping company, one Evaline, soon to be —Easton.

YEARS LATER, MANY YEARS PAST EVEN MR. SHAW'S predictions, the dear Uncle passed away. His funeral was well attended, much more so than his house party. And the guests present were those from all stations, all levels of wealth and success. Each person had been touched by Mr. Shaw in one way or another. As they listened to the words of praise for his life, Eva and Oscar fought their own tears of sorrow and gratitude. They'd received notice that a large portion of his shipping business, including his incredible fleet of ships, had been left to Oscar. And the ornaments on his Christmas tree, all his most precious and dear memories, had been left to Eva. Neither knew which gift meant more.

The End

Follow Jen

Jen's other published books

The Nobleman's Daughter
Two lovers in disguise

Scarlet
The Pimpernel retold

A Lady's Maid
Can she love again?

His Lady in Hiding
Hiding out at his maid.

Spun of Gold
Rumpelstilskin Retold

Dating the Duke
Time Travel: Regency man in NYC

Charmed by His Lordship
The antics of a fake friendship

Tabitha's Folly
Four over-protective brothers

To read Damen's Secret
The Villain's Romance

Follow her Newsletter

Chapter One: Snow and Mistletoe

❧

L ately, things were odd. Her mother hadn't left her bedroom in two weeks. Her father entertained untitled people from all walks of life. The servants were skittish. But no one would say anything at all about why.

Lady Theadosia Manet sat pondering the oddities with a book in hand, passing the time before calling hours. She'd like to be finishing her book. Another of Jane Austen's had just been published, and she had to finish the one in hand before she could begin the other. But the pages to her latest gothic novel were left unturned as her mind puzzled their situation. Could Father be working on another bill for Parliament? Could he be doing research? Could he be aiding the Bow Street Runners as he was sometimes wont? A maid bobbed a curtsey in front of her. "Your father would like to see you in his study."

Something in her throat tightened. A summons to Father's study usually meant pleasant conversation, but today the feelings of dread were surprising at the same time they were expected. Perhaps she could learn something that would explain their staying in London for Christmas, or the fact that her father didn't go to White's anymore, but stayed locked up in his study, receiving caller after caller.

She made her way through the rooms at the front of their home. Her fingers trailed on the backs of their furniture. Would things start to make sense around their home again? As soon as she entered the study, and Father looked as though he'd been up all night, nothing on his tea tray touched, she knew things were about to become even more strange. "What is it?"

He glanced up from what looked to be a well-read letter, the folds growing worn. "Come in. Sit."

She did, but only just. Her backside barely covered the corner of the chair, her legs poised to rise.

While dipping his pen in ink, he began. "Lord Standish has asked for your hand."

She nearly spit in surprise. "In marriage?"

"Yes, Dosie." His neat hand penned more words. "That's generally what asking for a hand entails."

"Was he overly disappointed when you refused?"

Father didn't meet her eyes.

"You did refuse him, didn't you?"

"Not...precisely." He finally looked up from his work.

"Father, you must do so, and sooner rather than later. I can't have the man thinking he can come call, follow me about at the balls and such."

"I'm not certain refusing him is the best decision."

"How can you say that? Would *you* want to live with him? He's as pale as the dead. He...he looks unhappy all the time. The man scowls." She shivered.

"Hardly reasons to dismiss him outright."

She couldn't believe the words that were entering her

ears. Dosie shook her head. "I will turn him down." But her father kept talking.

"We could do really well by him."

"We could do well by him?" She repeated her father's words hoping he would see how he sounded. Was he speaking of an offer of marriage or a business arrangement? Obviously the latter. "I feel cold whenever he's near. Real gooseflesh and not the pleasant kind."

"The weather has been...drafty."

"No Father, that's not it. He's...not a good man."

"He might be lovely. You don't know him very well."

"But I know him well enough. Father. What is this talk? We do not need to marry in haste. We can be selective, can't we? I don't wish to marry yet, and I certainly don't wish to marry him." She stood to emphasize her point, hoping her father would listen. "I will turn him down."

Her father's eyes, though resigned, held a certain glint to them and she wondered what the hurry was and why Lord Standish? Why this dreadful man of all the men?

"He is persuasive, that is all." Her father closed his ledger. "He comes to me with an offer I find difficult to refuse. He's extraordinarily connected, you know."

"With whom?" The man was an earl.

"His father will be appointed as the newest duke. He's meeting with Prinny this month. Lord Standish will soon be the most sought-after man in all of London, and you will have already captured him."

"And this new duke?"

"He's key to the balance of votes in Parliament. He is believed to be a Whig."

She stopped caring the minute votes and Parliament entered the discussion. But she knew her father had carefully drafted and argued and wrote papers on certain bills and efforts he hoped to move forward in the House of Lords and Commons. He was very active and cared deeply about his position there, sometimes to the exclusion of all else.

But he rubbed his forehead in resignation. "We will speak no more about it today."

"Have you been working on a bill lately? You've been so…distracted."

"Yes. Perhaps one of the most important of our day. It is coming together, remarkably, miraculously. But I need all the votes I can muster, all the assistance." He sighed. "I haven't even seen your mother these past weeks."

A servant scratched at the door.

"Come." Her father's voice sounded tired.

A maid entered with a curtsey. "Lady Theadosia has callers, my lord."

"Is it that time already?" She stood. "Thank you, Father. I really do wish to assist you in your pursuits. This must be of the utmost importance if you were to ask a marriage of me." She waited. But he was distracted once more, taking his quill up again. He looked up as if just remembering her presence. "Thank you. Enjoy your callers. The man himself is likely warming your front room furniture with all his coldness."

A certain growing concern stayed with her as she left his study and moved to the front room to receive callers. With any luck, Lady Jane would have already arrived.

She stood at the opened double doors to their front receiving parlor. Just as her father predicted, Lord Standish's dark presence had descended, and did she imagine things or did the temperature in the room drop? She shivered.

The footman announced, "Lady Theadosia Manet."

Everyone stood: two lords she quite enjoyed, her dear Lady Jane, and the ominous Lord Standish. She curtseyed, smiling at the room at large, avoiding looking too closely or deeply at Lord Standish.

Lady Jane gave her a look, the kind of look that meant, *oh I have things to say but I cannot say them.* And Dosie wished immediately that they were alone. But instead, she had the shy Lord Denning making eyes in her direction; the effervescent Lord Hamilton fanning his face; and the eerie Lord Standish sulking in the corner, so to speak. Hopefully she and Lady Jane would manage without Dosie's mother who had complained earlier of the nerves. What precisely were the nerves? Dosie had yet to learn. But her mother had them and therefore it was up to Dosie and Lady Jane to make the best of things.

Dosie began by pouring tea. "Tell me, Lord Denning. How is your mother?"

"Oh, she is well." He nodded four times before continuing. "Well indeed."

"Excellent, and Lord Hamilton."

"Hm?"

"I am admiring your cravat from here. Is that a pattern I see in the folds?"

He lifted his chin. "Yes, you are the first to comment." He eyed the men on either side before continuing. "The fabric itself has been stamped with ducks. It reminds me of the Hamilton hunt that happens every year at our house party. You will be attending, will you not?" He looked most specifically at Lady Jane, which Dosie found amusing. She liked Lord Hamilton. And she would be pleased if he could find a good match. Lady Jane would be highly entertained by him all her days. Wouldn't be the worst match. Unlike Lord Standish, who would undoubtedly be the worst match as far as overall congeniality.

"We are attending." Dosie nodded. "Will you also be attending, Lord Denning?"

He bumbled for a moment, looking this way and that until at last he said, "Yes."

Lord Standish shifted in his seat. "I, too, shall be attending. Although, I wonder if I might see you, Lady Theadosia, at the ball tonight?"

"Is there a ball tonight?" She tapped her chin, although she knew very well that there was indeed a ball, one she most desperately wished to attend, one that she and Lady Jane had been discussing for weeks.

"Quite. The Dansford ball." His expression remained placid, intense yet at the same time bored looking. How he managed such a feat was beyond her, but the result was unnerving.

"Oh yes, the very one. Yes. We will both be attending."

He opened his mouth to ask for her first set. She could see it on his lips, hear the words before they were uttered. She pinched Lady Jane.

"Lord Standish!" Her voice, blurting though it was, had the desired effect. He turned his attention to her. She started for a moment as though at a loss for words. Lord Standish had that effect with his tall, overly thin frame and his long pointed nose. The pallor of his skin, though much admired in the ladies, gave him an ethereal effect. He belonged in a gothic novel. But despite all of that raven-like eeriness looking down upon her, Lady Jane rallied. "Um. You see. I was wondering if you had heard any news from your sister?"

Remarkable. What a glorious friend Lady Jane was. His

sister had moved to India with her new husband. Excellent conversation. Safe as well.

And as predicted, he talked for many minutes about India, about the heat, the animals, the smells and how his sister was doing everything she could not to brown her skin. But to no avail, apparently she was particularly freckled.

"There's no need for a person to become weathered." Lord Hamilton shuddered.

"Well now, perhaps I am a bit of a different duck, but I do think some sun on the cheeks can add something to a complexion, no?" Dosie looked to Lady Jane for her support but she shook her head. "Not this Lady. I don't get a lovely pink rouge. I freckle. And they are impossible to lose."

Lord Standish continued. "She says the monkeys are adorable. She hopes to bring one home to London when they return and that the food is delicious, especially the fruits."

They talked for many minutes on the lack of fruit in London this season and then the hours for calling had come to a close. Lady Jane and Lady Theadosia stood. "Thank you for coming." Lady Theadosia offered her hand to each as they moved past toward the door. Lord Standish waited a moment before he approached, presumably so that fewer were in the room. "I would like to beg your hand for the first set of the dance."

"Of course." She curtseyed. "Thank you for coming today."

He stepped closer and lowered his voice. "Perhaps your father has spoken to you?" His eyebrow rose, but in his case the effect was so much less appealing and more of a demanding sort of question that Lady Theadosia wanted nothing more than to deny any conversation had taken place.

But honesty prevailed. "Yes, we have spoken."

"I look forward to spending more time at your side."

She held up a hand. "Before you say more, you must know that I have not accepted a courtship, nor any other more formal arrangement. I am much more comfortable leaving such things undecided for now."

His mouth straightened into a line, and Lady Jane shivered beside her. At least Dosie wasn't the only one to be so affected by this rather singularly unappealing man. But he bowed and said only, "I look forward to our set."

"Thank you."

He left, but the coldness that oft travelled in his wake lingered.

Chapter Two: Snow and Mistletoe

Julian Easton studied the odds of all the horses about to race. Cherry Picker was widely considered the first choice to win. Which meant he was going to bet against her. Everyone knew that you could win big doing things that way. And Cherry Picker couldn't win every single race of the day. It just wasn't possible. He put everything in his pocket down on the horse most predicted to lose. Nodded, satisfied with his potential, he made his way to the stands to watch the races.

Tauney had come, but only because Julian had forced him to. The man had no interest in wagers, betting, horse races or gambling in any way. Which Julian found odd. But he was the best of brothers and the only one who had nothing else to do.

"I think you have good odds with Cherry Picker."

"I didn't bet on her."

"What? Why not? I thought we were coming here because she was the one horse who couldn't lose? Everyone says it. Guaranteed return so you can pay back Edward?"

Tauney's expression filled Julian with doubts about his last-minute rash decision.

"Look, I know what I'm doing. I've been studying this stuff for weeks."

"And losing for weeks."

"Not today." He shook his head. "I feel good about this."

"Do I want to know who you bet on?"

He shook his head. "Bad luck. I'll tell you when he wins."

Tauney flicked a piece of dust from his jacket. "I don't know how this place is always so dirty."

Julian shrugged. He never minded a bit of dirt. He'd enjoy working on the estate if they were home. London life was confining for him. But the races made up for that.

The gun fire started the first race. Julian's horse wouldn't come up until the fourth. "You ever going to marry, Tauney?"

"If Edward has anything to do with it, I will."

"He's like...what is he like? I've never seen a brother harp on his siblings so much."

"I think he means for us to be happy." Tauney grimaced.

"Hmm."

They sat in silence for a minute, cheering or moans of disappointment as their backdrop. Then Tauney turned to him. "I'll marry. I'd like a family."

"Me too, someday." Julian did wish to marry, but with what? Where would he live? On what money? Perhaps these gambling ventures would pay off at last and he could start putting money down on an estate. "I'd like to be a landholder."

"Would you?" Tauney's raised eyebrows raised so much

doubt that Julian had to call him on it. "You don't believe me?"

"I believe you. But you throw away a lot of money for one who wants to buy an estate."

"I'm trying to win it back. I've just got to pay off Edward and some creditors and then I'm free and clear to put the funds aside. I'd like to live near the Easton estate."

Tauney nodded. "Excellent idea."

The announcer called, "Cherry Picker. Running Sands." The other names meant nothing. This was the race. Julian leaned forward.

"Is your horse in this race?"

He nodded.

The gun went off and the horses broke out onto the racetrack. At first Cherry Picker was in the lead. She'd been racing ahead and staying ahead for every race of the day. And it looked like she might do the same again. Julian clenched his fists.

But then Running Sands started to pick up the pace. He gained ground, passing one horse after another. One lap to go and he was still passing the others one at a time until they were in the finishing stretch and he was gaining on Cherry Picker.

Everyone in the stands stood. Julian bit the inside of his mouth. But then he couldn't resist. "Come on Running Sands!!" He shouted.

Tauney looked at him with mouth open. "You bet on Running Sands?"

"Yes, and look at him!"

The horse ran faster and closer, catching up until it was even with Cherry Picker, who was in the clear lead. At last, with barely a second to spare, Running Sands broke ahead and they crossed the finish line.

Julian jumped up and down. Tauney sat back, seemingly stunned. Everyone else in the stands fell back in a dejected heap. If no one else bet on Running Sands, Julian had won big, indeed.

"Today is my lucky day, Tauney. That's enough to get me started."

He clapped Julian on the back. "You, brother, are one lucky gentleman."

He chuckled as he made his way down to the betting boxes. He really had won big. He could win even bigger. This money would pay off his creditors, sure, but wouldn't put him ahead in saving for an estate. Perhaps he should try a little more of his luck.

Instead of cashing in his winnings, Julian turned it back in to bet on Running Sands again in his next race.

Humming, he returned to his seat.

"How much?" Tauney leaned close.

"Nearly two thousand pounds."

"What! That's incredible."

"I know. Watch it triple. I put it all up on Running Sands for his next race."

"You did what!" Tauney stood, his face equal parts shock and anger.

"Like I said, I've been doing this a long time."

Tauney didn't say anything more but he was clearly unhappy.

Race after race, they talked of small unimportant things until the last race of the day. Running Sands was up against the other winners from earlier races.

"Here we go. Tauney this is where you see the Julian magic."

At the gun, the horses tore out of their boxes. Running Sands took up the last spot. And Julian waited for him to start overtaking horses like he had earlier. He waited for one lap, then two, then three. "Come on, Running Sands!"

But the horse fell further behind for one lap, two, then three. And Julian knew he'd made the biggest gambling mistake of his life.

Not wanting to look at Tauney, he closed his eyes and listened to the announcer call the winner—not Running Sands. He couldn't say easy come easy go. He couldn't feel fine about it. A great feeling of waste descended. What was he doing here in the first place?

"What an incredible waste of time." Julian stood. "Come on, Tauney. Sorry I made you witness that."

Tauney said nothing but followed his brother through the stands and outside of the racing grounds.

The happy faces of people counting money surrounded him, but he pushed through it. "I've got to stop this."

Tauney's hand on his shoulder said more than any word could. It was there supporting, forgiving, even condemning with love—and Julian especially appreciated all of the words not spoken. Surely he would hear all those words later from Edward's mouth.

They stopped at White's, mostly to avoid returning home to Edward who no doubt had already heard or would hear of Julian's incredible waste of money.

The men's club was crowded, more so than usual. Perhaps Julian had made some money on his bets in the book. Every little bit helped at this point.

But it took almost a quarter hour to get a look at the book. Something must be going on of great interest in the ton. When at last he opened its pages, he saw his friend Lady Theadosia's name. And her father. He was trying to push forward a Whig agenda. People were betting who the woman would marry. Everyone picked a Whig supporter, someone of influence in the Parliament, or other such type. Julian shook his head. If Lady Theadosia had anything to say about it, and knowing her as he did, she would have much to say, she wouldn't be marrying a single one of the cads on that list. They'd met as children, their families often taking dinner together, and had become fast friends. She was singularly the most independently minded woman of his acquaintance.

He turned to Tauncy. But he'd lost his brother.

Beau Brummell himself had just entered the club. Tauncy gravitated to him like most of the others and would be listening to every word for as long as the fashion paragon chose to stay and speak.

Julian found a place in the corner. Perhaps he should alert Lady Theadosia that she and her father's dealings were so openly discussed.

Lord Standish entered. Julian knew very little of him, but he drew the eye. A bit odd in the manner of his dress but more especially in that the man never smiled. Julian nodded in his direction and received barely a tip of the head in return.

Several other lords joined Julian and with the great fuss over Beau Brummell, no one paid any attention to Lord Standish and his group. But one of the men slipped some coin, a full bag by the looks of it, into Standish's hands.

Keenly interested in any passage of coin, Julian pondered their small group for many minutes. Certainly no good was coming of their goings on. But coin. Julian could use some coin. He was about to stand and make his way over to them when Tauncy laughed overly loud.

Their group of fashion frenzied men would be going on for many hours. And Standish and his group had already slipped away when he turned back to them. He sighed. No other table held anyone of interest to him, and he had no desire to learn the latest knot for his cravat. It was time for him to make his way home.

Tauney nodded to his brother's farewell.

Julian stepped outside onto St. James Street with no particular direction and not feeling especially motivated to try to think of one.

READ the rest HERE

Lords for the Sisters of Sussex Series

The Duke's Second Chance

The Earl's Winning Wager

Her Lady's Whims and Whimsies

Suitors for the Proper Miss

Pining for Lord Lockhart

The Foibles and Follies of Miss Grace

Follow Jen's Newsletter for a free book and to stay up to date on her releases. https://www. subscribepage.com/y8p6z9

Chapter 1 The Earl's Winning Wager

❧❦❧

Morley stared at his best friend, waiting for the man to look up from his cards. Gerald was losing terribly. And Morley wasn't sure if he should feel guilty or victorious. His friend had just thrown most of a new inheritance from his distant cousin on the table, almost as if he wished to give it away.

Despite Gerald being the Duke of Granbury with significant holdings to his name, Morley wasn't comfortable taking so much—even in something as unbiased as a card game. But his friend smiled so large it looked like his cheeks hurt. Morley's hurt just looking at him.

"How can you smile when you're losing abominably?" Lord Morley frowned at him.

"I have leave to be happy so soon after my own wedding."

"But you don't have leave to gamble away your living, even to your best friend."

"I'm hardly close to losing a living."

Lord Morley raised his eyebrows. The other lords at the

table stared greedily at the back of Gerald's cards. But even though Lord Morley shook his head, none too subtly, Gerald pushed all the remaining chips and his slips of paper into the center.

"Included in this are some holdings in the south."

Lord Morley narrowed his eyes.

Gerald fanned out his cards. "Good, but"—he smiled even broader—"not good enough." Then each of the men laid out their cards. Gerald beat Lord Oxley soundly, as Morley suspected he knew he would. Then Lords Harrington and Parmenter threw their cards down. That left Morley's cards. Morley had won. Gerald knew he'd won. He eyed him above his cards. "What is this about?"

"Lay out your cards, man. On with it." Gerald's smile couldn't grow any larger, and even though Morley had just grown significantly more wealthy, he didn't trust his oldest friend.

Morley fanned out his cards and narrowed his eyes. "What are you doing?"

Gerald tipped his glass back and drained its contents. "Losing to my best friend. Come now. It's time for us to return home. Her Grace wants me home early."

"How is she feeling?"

Gerald's face clouded, and Morley regretted the question. Since the man had lost his first wife during childbirth, the prospect of doing it all over again loomed in his mind at all hours. Morley talked to him of it often enough. "She seems in the very prime of health. No one has looked healthier."

"No need to speak optimism in my ear. I know she is well, but then, so was Camilla. All we can do is wait and see. Amelia so wanted a child, and I love my wife too much to leave her alone. So there we have it."

Morley clapped him on the back as they stepped out of White's. "Do you ever consider it odd that when youth, we used each other's titles in preparation for the moment the great weight would fall on our shoulders? And now. You still call me Morley, but I ... don't call you anything but Gerald." He laughed trying to lighten the mood.

"You will always be Morley. Even your mother calls you Morley." He laughed. "Why is that?"

"I couldn't guess. Maybe she loves the title?" He shrugged. "Now, enough mystery. Tell me, what did I just win? What's this all about? These holdings in the south?"

"Remember our visit to Sussex?"

Morley half nodded, and then he stopped dead in the street. "When we went to save you from Lady Rochester? And we paid a visit to a family of ladies?" His eyes narrowed. Unbidden, Miss Standish's face came into his mind. "What did you do?"

"I inherited their castle, if you recall."

"I recall a heap of rubble with a few standing rooms."

"Well, we've been fixing it up, and the ladies are just about ready to move in. Five women, all of age. June, the eldest, is not quite twenty three, the youngest sixteen. You won the whole lot of them, with some other holdings besides. The winnings should cover the remaining repairs and upkeep for a time as well."

"I won't take it."

"You have no choice. There were witnesses."

Morley was silent for so long he hoped Gerald began to half suspect he'd truly overstepped his generosity at long last. Then he shook his head. "I know what you're doing, and she doesn't want anything to do with me."

"I don't know what you're talking about."

"And she will want even *less* to do with me if she thinks

she is in any way beholden to me, so whatever plans you have going, you can just take back your properties and your pesky family of women and leave me in peace."

"Morley, you're my oldest and best friend. Would I really foist these women on you if I didn't think it would make you the happiest of men? They're from the Northumberland line. Excellent family heritage. The Queen herself takes an interest in their well-being."

"I care not for any of such nonsense, and you know it. You are not to be a matchmaker. It doesn't suit you. And you're terrible at it."

"How would you know, since I've never attempted such a roll until now?"

"So you admit it?"

"I admit nothing. Now, come, don't be cross. You'll upset Amelia."

"Oh, that is low, bringing your wife's condition into this."

They stepped into the townhome, where Simmons took their hats and gloves and overcoats. Gerald waved Morley in. "Thank you for staying with us while you're in town."

"At times, I prefer your home to my own situation."

"You're a good son, though."

Morley hoped he was, though his mother was tiring at best and liked to have her fingers in most aspects of his dealings. He loved her, and felt she was happy in her life, such as it was.

A soft, melodic voice called, "Gerald? Is that you?"

Amelia stepped out into the foyer. "And Morley." She clapped her hands, and the smile that lit her face filled the room.

He accepted her kiss on the cheek and watched as Gerald turned all of his focus to his wife.

Morley bowed. "I will bid you good night. Tomorrow, Gerald, we will discuss your sneaking ways."

"What has he done?" Amelia could only look with love at the Duke, and Morley felt, for a moment, a pang of loneliness.

"I've done nothing. Morley is just a sore winner."

Morley refused to say more. He bowed to Amelia and made his way up the stairs. Before he reached the first landing, he turned. "Oh, and Gerald?"

Gerald turned from his wife for a brief moment.

"When are we to go visit my winnings?"

"Oh, you're on your own with that one, Morley. They will much prefer you to me at any rate." He turned back to Her Grace, and Morley continued up the stairs, his mood darkening with every step.

Gerald had gone too far—in some mad effort to match him with a woman who really had no more interest in Morley than she did dancing a quadrille. June Standish was as practical as he'd seen a person.

He sighed.

And far handsomer than any he'd yet laid eyes on. Her hair was gold—it looked to be spun from the metal itself—and her eyes large, doe-like. He had lost all sense of conversation when he first saw her. It had taken many minutes for him to gain his faculties enough to speak coherently, but she had seemed entirely unaffected. And so that was it for them.

He could only imagine her reaction when he returned to let her know a new gentleman, he himself, was now lord over her life and well-being. Gerald should not toy with others' lives. He needed to be stopped. But Morley wasn't going to be the one to stop him. They'd carried on in their friendship in just this way since they'd known each other.

Perhaps he could appeal to Amelia. She had more control over the man than anyone.

What did he need with a decrepit, dilapidated castle? It was an old seat of the royal dukes, so there was a certain level of prestige associated with the place—and with the women. They were of the ancient Normandy family lines. Someone somewhere in their family had wasted their money and left nothing for the line to live off of, but it was still considered an elevated situation if you were on friendly terms with any of the Sisters of Sussex, as they were called.

Sleep did not come easily, and morning was not friendly to Morley's tired eyes and mind. Instead of breaking his fast with Gerald and Amelia, he left for a walk. Oddly, his steps took him to Amelia's old tearoom. They let it out, once she was to become the duchess, and someone else ran the establishment instead. As he stood in the doorway, he almost walked away without entering. What was he doing in a tearoom? Colorful dresses filled the shop to bursting.

"Lord Morley!" With the swish of skirts, a woman's hands were on his arm. "What a pleasant surprise. You must join us for tea. We are discussing the upcoming McAllister ball."

He allowed himself to be led to their table, and when four expectant female eyes turned their hopeful expression toward him, he could only smile and say, "How perfect, for I was just wondering about the details."

"Then you are attending?" Lady Annabelle's eyes lit with such a calculating energy, he shifted in his seat, eyeing the door for a second.

"I am, indeed."

"How provident. Then we shall all be there together. You remember we all became acquainted at the opera one week past. Miss Talbot, Miss Melanie—"

"And Lady Annabelle. Naturally, we are acquainted. It is a pleasure to see you again. I hope your mother is well?"

Lady Annabelle poured his tea, and his mind could not leave the family he'd just won charge of. What sort of women was this new family of sisters? He'd been most impressed with them when considering them as Gerald's wards, of a sort. But now that he owned the house they lived in, he felt a whole new interest in their deportment. Could they pour a man's tea? Stand up well with the other ladies at a ball? Would he be able to marry them off? That was the crux of it. And dash it all, why must he be concerned with the marrying off of anyone? He was in over his head. He needed help. He could appeal to Amelia's sense of grace, but she would have little knowledge of the ways of the *ton*.

The women chattered around him, and he almost sloshed his tea in the saucer when he heard mention of the very women who so aggravated his thoughts.

"They call them the Sisters of Sussex."

"Really? Who are they?"

"The Duke of Northumberland's relations, from a royal line. They are the talk of the *ton* and favorites of many of the noble families. We ourselves have stopped by with some of last season's gowns."

"Five sisters, you say? And they live in the old castle?"

"A cottage nearby. The castle is being renovated, though. I heard the Duke of Granbury has become involved." Lady Annabelle turned to him. "Do you know much about the sisters?"

He cleared his throat and shifted in his seat. "I have met them."

The other ladies leaned forward, eyes on him.

"And I found them charming," he said. "I think you

know more about their history than I. Though I do know the castle will be repaired and livable, as it deserves to be. It's a remarkable structure."

Miss Talbot fanned her face. "I should like to visit. I love old buildings and their architecture."

"Do you?" Morley tipped his head to her. She was a pretty sort of woman. Chestnut curls lined her face, and deep brown eyes smiled at him.

"Yes, I like to draw them, and then study them after."

"Interesting. Perhaps we shall meet up there sometime."

"Oh?" Lady Annabelle rested a hand on his arm. "Will you be spending much time in Brighton?"

He hadn't planned on it yet. He'd hoped to stay as far away as possible until his mind wrapped around this new responsibility. But he changed his plans in the moment. "I think I shall." He looked into each of their faces. They were pleasant women. They seemed kind—unassuming, perhaps. "Might I ask for some assistance?"

"Certainly." Lady Annabelle's eyes gleamed.

"I wonder, if I were to assist the ladies—any ladies—to be prepared for a smallish Season in Brighton, do they have a dressmaker or shops enough down there?"

"Oh, certainly. Not nearly as grand or varied as London, but a woman can make do with what Brighton has to offer. The Brighton Royal Pavilion has brought much of the *ton* and a higher level of prestige to the area."

"Thank you."

Their gossip-loving ears seemed to perk right up and all three pairs of eyes looked on him a bit too keenly. He resisted adjusting his cravat. "So, who will be attending the McAllister ball? And have each of you found partners already for your dances?"

The chatter grew more excited, and they listed all the

people who were coming or might be coming, depending on the attendance of others. He lingered as long as was polite, and then excused himself from this cheery group.

He would go check in on his mother, though he planned not to mention his new winnings at the table, and then make arrangements to travel down to visit the Standish sisters. God willing, he could establish good solutions for their situation and living and have them well in hand within a few weeks.

Chapter 2 The Earl's Winning Wager

❦

Miss June Standish ran her finger down the ledger, calculating expenses, the infernal drafts in the cottage sending a trail of gooseflesh up her arms. She pulled her thickest shawl tighter around her shoulders. The hour was early yet. None of her sisters had ventured downstairs, but their remaining in bed might have more to do with the chill in the air than them being asleep. Though she assumed her youngest sister, Grace, continued to sleep soundly.

They could probably burn more wood. They had a budget for it. Ever since the Duke of Granbury inherited their cottage and castle, things had improved. But they didn't have enough servants to get the fire going in the morning. And the way she looked at it, once you left your bed, you may as well venture downstairs to be in the kitchen where it was warmest anyway. Perhaps they should hire another servant.

The castle renovations were under way. She wasn't certain she wanted to move with her sisters into another infernally drafty place, but His Grace had assured her the living areas of the castle would be superior to her current situation. They were scheduled to move in next month.

He had also assured her that her chances of marrying would improve if they lived in the castle. Anyone who didn't know their royal connections would be made aware, simply by their inhabiting the old seat.

She sighed. If only she could see each of her sisters happily married.

Grace stepped into the kitchen, her blankets wrapped around her.

June stood. "Grace, what are you doing up so early?"

"I couldn't sleep. This house makes noises."

"We've been here long enough for you to know the noises don't mean a thing."

"They have to mean something. I was more worried about them when we first arrived, but I'll admit, sometimes I see an old, weathered sailor with absurdly long fingernails scratching on my window."

"Goodness. You do have an imagination."

Grace shrugged and sat as close to June as she could. "What are you working on?"

"I'm determining if we need another servant."

"A lady's maid?"

June laughed. "And what do we need one of those for?"

"To do our hair, help us dress…"

"We have each other."

"But a maid could do the modern styles, help us look our very best. His Grace said we'd be having a Season."

"The others will. You are still too young to be out."

She groaned in frustration. "Really, am I too young for everything?"

"No, you are just the right age to help me get some water boiling."

"A cook. We should hire another assistant for cook."

June had thought of it. "I think the castle has its own staff as well, so when we blend there, we can work out different responsibilities among the staff. It's just one more month."

Grace grinned. "I can't wait. I love the castle. And then no one can forbid me to enter or explore, because we will all live there."

"That is true. There will be areas blocked off for safety reasons while the renovations continue, but we shall have a rather large area that is our own living space."

"Do you think this is what Uncle wanted for us?"

"Perhaps." June toyed with her quill. They had all loved their uncle, the Earl of Beaufort, as old and confused as he sometimes became. He had swept in and picked up the pieces of their broken lives, hugged the loneliness out of them, and helped them feel centered and loved. His loss was one of their greatest, almost to the intensity of losing their parents. "Regardless of his intent, we are making the best of it, are we not?"

"Yes. I'm just grateful we have each other." She curled closer and rested her head on June's shoulder.

"I feel the same, sweet." She tipped her head so it rested on the top of Grace's. They sat thus for a moment more. Then June knew it was time to begin the day. "We have our studies this morning. And our dancing instruction this afternoon."

"Will we ever have a man to practice with?"

"Someday, when we dance the real thing." June laughed. "Am I not a good enough dance partner?"

"You're excellent." Grace's tone and expression said just the opposite.

"I hope one day to see you all happily wed. You know that. Perhaps with the duke's help, we can secure good matches for each one of you."

"And you." Grace's large and caring eyes made June's heart clench.

"You are a dear, but I might feel happiest just to see each one of you settled."

"And perhaps one of us will marry gobs of money, enough to care for us until our dying days."

"That would be wonderful, but the only thing I ask is you also marry for happiness."

Grace nodded. "But don't you think all manner of happiness could be found, if the living is comfortable?"

"I suppose." June didn't wish to fill her sister's head with romantic fancies. For a woman in the Standish sisters' financial state could not afford to be romantic in her choice of marriage partner. But they could insist on happiness, on comfort or security. She hoped they could at least strive for that.

After a modest breakfast, all five sisters met in the music and school room. June smiled at them all. Every now and then, she had to relax about their many worries and just appreciate the good that surrounded them. Grace, Lucy, Kate, and Charity were the best of women, the very best she knew, at any rate, and she was intensely proud of every one.

They'd converted an additional sitting room to their place of projects. On one end, the easels were set, with large, billowing fabric covering the floor to catch the paint. They had a pianoforte, a smaller harp, needlepoint, and on the other end of the room, a large blackboard and a bookshelf full of books. Their library might be small compared to some, but it was full of June's most prized possessions.

As the only Standish daughter who'd had a governess, and she for only a short amount of time, June spent an hour every day working on their deportment, the rules of society, their manners, and their general instruction in the ways of a gently bred lady.

"And what if I do not wish for a gently bred man?" Charity's stubborn streak grew the longer they lived in Sussex. June wasn't sure what drove her stronger sensibilities.

"I just want you happy, and in most cases, that means with enough food on the table, an established place to live, and a good man. If that can be found in the working classes, then all the happier I will be, since you profess to prefer such a life."

"'Such a life.' What a snob you are, June."

"Tsk. She's not a snob." Kate shifted her skirts. "She does well by us to show us how to present ourselves. I, for one, do not wish to be embarrassed when next the Duchess of York stops in."

"Oh, she is the utmost. That woman's nose is so far in the air, I'm surprised she can walk." Charity shook her head.

"We are grateful for their goodness to us. All our fine dresses come from her and the others."

"Yes." Kate slumped in her seat. "Last year's fashions."

"And still plenty ostentatious." Charity lifted her skirts. "Who needs embroidery on the hem? Lace I can see, but embroidery? It just gets dirty on these roads and is impossible to wash out."

"Then don't be wearing the embroidery while out

exploring the dirty roads." Kate poked her needle into the handkerchief she was sewing.

"What are you making?" June leaned closer.

"I'm hoping to have a stack of these for when we go to dinners and balls in Brighton. Then a man could know where to return it." She'd sewn pretty flowers on the edges, as well as her initials and Northumber Castle.

"That's lovely." June lifted her book. "Now, allow me to finish." She read to them from Shakespeare, and had more interest than in her previous descriptions of the early royal lineage. They would follow up the literature lesson with French, and then lunch.

In a break in her reading, Grace piped up, "We'll have dancing this afternoon."

"Do we have Jacques to come instruct us?" Charity's hopeful expression gave June pause.

"No, not today. We will be working on the country dances. And those are simple enough to memorize without Jacques. He will come next week for the waltz."

"Oh, I love the waltz." Grace clapped her hands together.

"As do I." Kate put down her embroidery, her black, shiny curls bouncing at her neck. "Do you think we could have a new bonnet for the promenade on Tuesday?"

"What promenade?" June searched her memory for mention of a promenade.

"Oh, come, June. Pay attention. Prinny will be back in town, and everyone will begin walking up and down the green. Everyone who is here will attend. It is the prime location for us to be seen and make an impression." She paused in a rather dramatic manner. "*If* we make a good impression."

"I wish to make a good impression. Do you think we

need new bonnets?" Grace looked from June to Kate and back.

"I think we will make the best impression, no matter what kind of bonnets are on our heads." June set the book aside. But inside she worried about just such a thing. Would they be able to be seen as anything other than charity to the gentry? Perhaps a bonnet would help? She shook her head. Everything seemed so overwhelming at times. She'd never had a Season herself. Her parents had fallen ill, and were taken from them around the time she would have started to prepare. What did she really know about any such thing? "No matter what, we must be a Standish daughter, women with a heritage to be proud of."

Stenson stepped into their small parlor. "The Duchess of Sussex here to see you."

June sucked in her breath. The arrival of the Duchess was a mixed blessing. "You know how we must receive her."

They all stood taller, painted blank expressions on their faces, and moved to the front sitting room, reserved almost solely for visits from the nobility—and in this case, the royal family. As soon as they were situated, each with a different manner of amusement—embroidery, reading, drawing, and two opposite a chess board, though no one had moved a single piece in ages—Stenson opened their door. "The Duchess of Sussex."

The Standish sisters stood and curtsied.

Their guest smiled, and her eyes twinkled. "Oh, my lovelies, my dears. Let me have a look at you." She held out her hands. She kept such a youth and vigor about her, June had vowed to do the same. Kate admired her clothing. Lucy coveted her title, and Charity looked at her with great suspicion.

JEN GEIGLE JOHNSON

June curtseyed again. "It is good to see you, Your Grace. You do us honor by your visit."

"I find so much happiness aiding in your situation, such as it is." She studied them for a moment, and June wondered if she'd break out in tears right then. "Oh, and aren't you the most deserving." She placed hands on her heart. "To think, so reduced in situation, so noble in bearing. You are all to be commended for your fortitude."

"Thank you, Your Grace." June dipped her head. "Would you care for some tea? Coffee?"

"Oh, thank you, if you can spare some."

"We have ample." June nodded to their maid, who waited just outside the door.

As soon as Her Grace was seated, she adjusted her skirts. They flowed in an elegant manner to the floor. The delicate flowers that lined her hemline, the tiny sparkles of gems which glittered when the sun touched them, must have been fascinating to June's most fashion-conscious sister, Kate.

"Has the Duchess of York been by?" The Duchess of Sussex asked, as though she didn't care, but June knew their answer would pester and bother her for days.

And Charity did too. "She has, and she brought us the most exquisite gowns. They must have been her own, they were so lovely. To everyone who asks, we must positively gush about the Duchess of York and her deep generosity."

"Oh, did she? That's nice, isn't it? Hmm." She narrowed her eyes and waved her hand. A servant in the Sussex livery appeared in the doorway as if summoned from invisibility. "Please bring in the packages."

He nodded.

"Well, I have brought some of my own."

Kate gasped and placed hands at the side of her face.

"Oh, thank you, Your Grace, for your sense of style is exquisite. I have been studying just now how perfectly you wear your clothing. Of all the ladies, you are my most favorite."

The duchess beamed. "I appreciate a woman who understands the finer details of fashion. Which one are you?" She lifted a quizzing glass. "Come here."

Kate almost tripped over herself to rush to Her Grace's side.

"Ah, yes. Miss Kate, is it?"

"Yes, Your Grace. If it pleases you."

"You shall have my brooch."

Their sister Lucy gasped, but June waved her to hush.

"Thank you." Kate's curtsy was low and grateful.

"I have brought dishes as well, and some food from cook's kitchen. We live near enough you should be recipients of our finest."

"Thank you. You could not dote upon more grateful servants."

"Now that we are here in Brighton for a smaller Season, I plan to visit often. Whenever we are in our Sussex estate, we will be sure to pay you a call."

"We will look forward to the honor."

The tea service arrived. "How would you like your tea?"

They ate and sipped, and the duchess filled them in on the gossip of the *ton* and from London.

"Oh, you sisters would love London. Imagine a Season in Town. Wouldn't that be so exciting! I cannot fathom how your forbearers could leave you with so little, so paltry your opportunities to attend such delights as a Season. I know a handsome earl. He would be perfect for one of you." She clucked. "A pity you could not go even one Season."

"Yes, pity." Charity's look of mock sorrow almost made June laugh, and she hoped the duchess would not see the duplicitous expression. Did the duchess not know the hurt her words could cause? Or did she really think the sisters didn't feel their situation keenly enough without her comments?

They chatted a few moments more and then bade the woman goodbye. She left piles of things in the entry. June should be grateful for the gifts, and she was. But unless the gowns fit, it was an expense to alter them, or a lot of work for the sisters. Kate was becoming quite proficient with a needle.

After lunch, and once the duchess departed, the sisters gathered back in the music room. Grace sat at the piano. "But I wish to dance this time. Someone give me a chance to practice the steps."

"We will, but after the rest of us have a go. You're the youngest."

"I know." Grace frowned. "So you all keep saying."

"Well, there is less a need for you to learn, as you won't even be dancing."

"Thank you, Lucy."

"We all know Lucy is going to marry money, and then the rest of us won't have to worry about getting married." Charity waved her hand in Lucy's direction.

"I'd like to get married." Kate pouted. "And so would everyone else, I imagine, including June."

"Yes, even me. But we'll worry about the rest of you first." She hid her sadness. *Even June.* She was not a spinster, not even close to being on the shelf, but she just didn't think she could spend the effort getting herself married when she had so many others to be concerned with.

Grace started in on a well-known country dance, and

June called out the steps while she did them. "You see? I start, and then I must add my own flair here. You watch and repeat."

The girls stepped together with imaginary partners, waited while their partners would have done the same, and then repeated. It was a bit confusing at times, but it worked well enough.

Then Stenson, their very young butler, stepped into the room. "A Lord Morley to see you."

The girls froze. Kate whispered, "Who?"

June's heart skipped, and the pause between beats thundered in her chest. "I—" Her voice cracked. "I do believe that is Morley?"

"The nice man who came with the duke? He's an earl?"

"Yes, he was introduced as such, but His Grace called him Morley so often, the 'earl' part didn't stick. I do hope we did not follow suit and omit his title." Lucy clucked. "To neglect to use a man's title without permission is an insult in the highest order."

"Yes, thank you, Lucy." June stood and straightened her dress, urging the girls to rise as well. They rolled the carpet back where it should be and patted down their hair. "Send him in, Stenson."

He nodded. "Very good, miss."

"Does anyone else think Stenson looks like a young boy playing a part?" Charity giggled.

"Hush." June shook her head.

And in walked Lord Morley, the man she'd thought of constantly since their meeting, the most handsome man of her albeit limited acquaintance. He filled the room with his large stature, his strong shoulders, his brilliant jawline, with the crisp white of his cravat brushing against it. His gaze flitted through the sisters and rested on June. And then the

corner of his mouth lifted in a soft smile. "Miss Standish."
He bowed. "Miss Charity, Miss Lucy, Miss Kate, and Miss
Grace."

Grace giggled from behind the piano.

They all curtsied.

Then June stepped forward. "We are so happy you have
come. Please, take a seat. Would you like some tea?"

"Tea would be wonderful, thank you."

Grace tripped off to the kitchen to inform their cook.

And June wasn't sure she could form words. Why had
he come? The idea he would arrive to pay a social call filled
her with hope, a hope she tried to tamp out.

"Tell us the news of London." Kate asked all their visi-
tors to talk of London. Usually she was most seeking news
of fashion, but as Lord Morley would likely know little of
those kinds of details, June supposed Kate would be satisfied with whatever snippets she could glean.

"Things are warming up in London, just enough to
almost be pleasant." He laughed. "Not many families
stayed on. I expect the Season to pick up in high form in a
month or two. I hear many of the families have come to
Brighton."

"We hear the same." Kate fluffed her skirts. "In fact, we
were just talking of doing a promenade on the green
tomorrow. Will you be staying long?"

"I will be here for a few weeks or more, I believe." His
gaze flitted to June's.

June didn't respond, for she wasn't sure what to say at
all to his statement. She was most desperately pleased, but
so impatient with herself for thinking in such a way. Charity
kicked her ankle. June started. "I'm happy to hear it. Would
you care to join us tomorrow in our promenade? Like Miss

Kate said, you are likely to see most everyone from Brighton at one point or another on the green."

"I should very much enjoy the outing, thank you."

The tea arrived, and June busied herself with the pouring. Why had he come? She couldn't account for it. And even though his gaze rested on her more than anywhere else, nothing could make sense in her mind as to why that would be.

READ THE REST HERE THE EARL'S WINNING WAGER

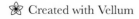

Made in the USA
Coppell, TX
08 January 2023